I0576623

SANDCASTLE FOR PEGASUS

BOB AVEY

Black Rose Writing | Texas

©2021, 2022 by Bob Avey

All rights reserved. No part of this book may be reproduced, stored in a retrieval system or transmitted in any form or by any means without the prior written permission of the publishers, except by a reviewer who may quote brief passages in a review to be printed in a newspaper, magazine or journal.

The author grants the final approval for this literary material.

Second printing

This is a work of fiction. Names, characters, businesses, places, events, and incidents are either the products of the author's imagination or used in a fictitious manner. Any resemblance to actual persons, living or dead, or actual events is purely coincidental.

ISBN: 978-1-68433-757-6
PUBLISHED BY BLACK ROSE WRITING
www.blackrosewriting.com

Printed in the United States of America
Suggested Retail Price (SRP) $19.95

Sandcastle for Pegasus is printed in Chaparral Pro

*As a planet-friendly publisher, Black Rose Writing does its best to eliminate unnecessary waste to reduce paper usage and energy costs, while never compromising the reading experience. As a result, the final word count vs. page count may not meet common expectations.

For my lovely wife, Kathi, who graciously shared her life with me,
but has now gone to be with the Lord.

Acknowledgements:

I would like to thank and acknowledge Emelia Monaghan for editing, Reagan Rothe with Black Rose Writing for believing in me, Christopher Miller for public relations support, the design team for the book cover, and the editing team for final editing.

SANDCASTLE
FOR PEGASUS

CHAPTER ONE

May 4, 2020, 11:00 a.m.

Martin Taylor's first thought was that he was dead. His parents had died in an automobile accident a few years ago, and now he was suffering the same fate.

His mind swirled, gathering and losing strength while he floated...in a tunnel that stretched about seven feet in diameter; the walls charged, with energy, electrical perhaps.

Martin dismissed the idea of death because...well...because he was here—wherever here was—and apparently cognizant on some level. He heard voices, though so nondescript he almost dismissed them as having no significance.

"Welcome to Camp Hero," the voices said.

Martin couldn't see anything. Whether that was because there was no light or because his eyes weren't working, he wasn't sure. He fancied momentarily that his mind had left his body to roam some mysterious realm, but that didn't seem right either. He wondered if he could be dreaming or—assuming the accident was real—if he was experiencing something much worse: he was trapped in a coma, his body stretched out on a bed in some hospital room.

He had seen the oncoming car. But he had failed, let everyone down as usual, and now he was tangled in a ton of twisted metal. And what about his son, Luke? Luke had been with him.

Martin tried to slow his racing heart. This could not be real! He wasn't dead. He tried to think other thoughts, anything but that. Like the fact that he was a good father and a good husband. Or like the fact that he had no confidence in himself. His whole life was one error or misjudgment after another. And now he'd really done it.

He and Luke were going to die.

A deep-rooted fear, an overpowering sense of helplessness, threatened to engulf Martin. He focused inward, gathered a moment of calm, and reflected on just how this might have happened. He remembered one of Grandma Phyliss's old sayings. She didn't have one for every occasion, only those she thought had mattered.

"Confidence is a tricky suit of clothing," she'd said. "Overplaying it can be detrimental, but underplaying it can be devastating."

●   ●   ●

As far as Martin could recall, it had all begun with Luke's doctor's appointment, but not with just any doctor. Doctor Jackson Stewart was a psychologist who specialized in brain mapping patients with autism and other mental disorders.

On the way home, Luke had grown quiet. Later, he shook his head. "I had another blowout with skates last night. I had it. I tired." Luke raised his elbow, which sported a nasty bruise. "I hurt myself. I through."

Martin kept his attention on the road. Luke's anger had risen along with his voice level, but that was Luke in a nutshell: sweet and loveable with a nasty little dose of Jekyll and Hyde lurking beneath the surface.

Roller skating was Luke's favorite outlet, and one of the few things he could do by himself. His sister, Krystal, had taught him. Krystal had always been a positive influence in Luke's life, and, still was, but she had her own life now.

Luke had asked for a new pair of skates for Christmas.

Martin had known Luke's heart hadn't been in the request. He'd been looking at riding mowers for several months, and that was what he'd really wanted. An extravagant gift, but Luke had gotten pretty good at lawn maintenance, and Martin both appreciated and depended on his help. Mowing grass in Oklahoma's summer heat was no picnic. During a moment of weakness, Martin had made a spur-of-the-moment decision to surprise Luke with a lawn mower, and he was glad he had. Finding the mower in the garage had made Luke beam with pride and joy—best Christmas ever.

But that had left the problem of the old skates unaddressed until Luke's birthday, which was today.

"I'm sorry about your arm," Martin said.

"It not your fault."

Martin smiled. He'd already ordered the skates and talked the manager of the rink into holding them. "I'll talk to Mom. Maybe we can go ahead and order the skates."

"What happens to trains without engines?"

Martin glanced to his left, where several boxcars were parked along the track, but kept most of his attention on the road. The traffic was heavy, but Luke seldom understood why Martin couldn't give him his full attention while he was driving. "They'll eventually get picked up."

"What about other trains? The train without an engine can't go. They might crash."

Luke's ramblings often seemed random and even nonsensical, but Martin had learned that a common thread usually existed. It might make sense only to Luke, but not always. "They probably won't crash. That used to happen, though rarely. But now, with computer systems and who knows what else, the companies probably know where everything is, trains and boxcars."

"What happens to trains without engines?"

Martin gripped the wheel of his car, an older Audi with a lot of miles. When Luke got circular with his questions, it usually meant something was bothering him. "Did anything happen during the doctor's visit that you're not telling me about?"

"Remember our vacation?"

Martin thought back. They'd gone to Panama City Beach, Florida. "Yeah, wish we were there now."

"We forgot the sandcastle."

Martin glanced at Luke, who was staring straight ahead as if studying the oncoming traffic. Luke hadn't asked about the songs on the radio. Martin loved classic rock, and Luke loved what Martin did. Luke often asked about the music, wanting to know who wrote a song and whether it was their first hit. But sandcastles? Luke had never brought up that subject.

They often vacationed in Florida. One thing they always did was build a sandcastle, except Martin usually did the building while Luke joined his mother looking for shells along the beach. They hadn't built one this year. Someone had been watching them at the pool, or so it had seemed to Martin—a tall man with dark hair and dark glasses—and again on the beach, the same man. Susan said it was probably nothing, just a coincidence, but it had made Martin uncomfortable.

"It's okay," Martin said. "We'll build two next year."

"I no go back."

An empty sensation built in Martin's stomach. "We can do something else. How about Colorado? That was fun."

"Doctor Stewart doesn't like me."

Martin fought for composure. He'd known something wasn't right the minute he and Luke had walked into Doctor Stewart's office. "What makes you think he doesn't like you? Did he tell you that?"

"He put me in a chair like Doctor Monroe does."

Doctor Monroe was Luke's dentist. Martin knew little about psychologists, but a dentist's chair? "What happened after that?"

"He put wires on me."

It was then that everything had come apart. Martin saw another vehicle, a black BMW, charge directly at them.

The road was open, and then it wasn't.

"What happening?" Luke asked, his voice quivering.

Martin had known that the head-on collision would smash both cars into unrecognizable hunks of metal and that he and Luke, in all probability, would not survive the crash.

Martin had been in accidents before, and everything was always a blur, but not this time. He saw the black BMW in amazing detail, as if he were watching a bizarre movie.

His last thought was that they were going to celebrate this weekend—a party for Luke and Susan. If Luke were killed, he would never get his skates.

It was then that everything had gone black.

CHAPTER TWO

May 4, 2020, 8:00 a.m.

Something touched Martin, a warm and soft hand upon his shoulder.

"Martin, wake up. You're going to be late."

He opened his eyes, letting them adjust to the light filtering into the room while his mind came out of a dream about Luke's doctor's appointment.

Susan's face showed concern. "You promised to take Luke to his appointment today, remember?"

Martin studied Susan's face, thinking—and not for the first time—just how lucky he was. "Happy birthday, my love."

"Thanks, but my birthday was yesterday."

"I know. I'm still celebrating." He leaned close, gave her a kiss on the cheek, and then rolled over, dropping his feet to the floor. After grabbing his phone from the nightstand, he strolled toward the bathroom but stopped halfway. It still seemed to him that he'd already taken Luke for his appointment yesterday. Turning back, he thought about telling Susan but changed his mind. It was a ridiculous notion. The appointment was scheduled for today.

"You were really thrashing around last night," she said, as if reading his mind. "You were talking, too. Couldn't make it out though. Never can."

The expression on Susan's face gave Martin more second thoughts. She was probably right, though he'd never confused a dream with reality. Even vivid and compelling dreams faded when he tried to remember them or put the imagery into words, but not this one. He recalled every detail, especially the look on the other driver's face. The man had not been frightened. If anything, he had been satisfied.

Martin wondered if he could be losing his mind. He turned back and continued into the bathroom, where he checked his phone.

Sure enough, it showed Monday, May 04.

Martin pulled an old watch from the drawer. He had inherited the watch—expensive by today's standards—from his grandfather. Martin loved the old timepiece, a large, heavy thing that was state-of-the-art in its time. It also showed May 04.

Martin thought back and remembered the long talks he had as a boy with his Grandpa Frank. Several times, his grandfather had brought up the concept of time travel. Martin hadn't really understood, so he had put the strange conversations out of his mind. However, he'd recently met a man named Tanner McIntosh, who was rather rough looking, but interesting. Much Like Martin's grandfather, Tanner was also fascinated by unusual things like time travel, though Martin had again put it on the back burner.

After showering and dressing, he strolled across the living room and into the kitchen. Glancing around, he said, "Watch it, Suze. Luke left one of his cars on the floor. You're about to step on it."

Susan shrieked. She kept a grip on the cup she carried, but the contents couldn't keep pace with her jerky movements and splashed to the floor.

"Damn it, Martin."

Martin grabbed a few paper towels and cleaned the spill. "I tried to warn you. And I thought we'd agreed not to use that kind of language."

Susan went to the table in the breakfast nook, where she plopped down into a chair, propped herself up with her elbows, and covered her face with her hands. "All right, all right. But you're leisurely going through the morning like it's a free Saturday or something. This is important."

Martin sat across from her, reached across the table, and gingerly pulled her hand away from her face. The company he worked for had recently changed insurance carriers, and the new insurance firm had asked for a psychological evaluation of Luke. "Sorry. Things are a bit crazy this morning. It's that silly dream. It has me rattled."

"Yeah," she said, "emphasis on *dream*. And you're going to be late."

"You're right," Martin said. He got up from the table and walked toward the hallway. He would have to wake Luke, and that was something both he and Susan tried to avoid. It was best to let Luke do that on his own. Martin paused at the door and gently rapped against it. He was surprised Susan's scream hadn't brought Luke out of his room. He eased the door open. "Hey, big guy. Mom has breakfast—that fancy oatmeal you like."

"I no go back."

Martin thought about that for a moment. It seemed a strange thing to say, even for Luke. "No," Martin said, "just this once. We won't have to do it again. I promise. And we have the birthdays coming up this week. That should be fun. I've invited Candy."

A few minutes later, they all sat around the table.

Susan kept checking her watch.

"They think I'm crazy?" Luke asked.

Martin exchanged a nervous glance with Susan. "No," he said, "nothing like that. It's just something we have to do for insurance."

"You and Mom not go."

Martin raised his coffee cup and drained it. "Sure, we did."

A white lie, but sometimes that was best with Luke. "Mom met me at work the other day, remember? We both went together before we came home."

Part of it was true. Susan had picked Martin up from work a few days earlier.

Luke's face went blank. Moments later he said, "Okay."

Martin breathed a sigh of relief. The day wasn't over, not by a longshot, but small victories were always good.

Luke moved the oatmeal, nuts, and raisins around with his spoon.

Martin found Luke's actions odd. Oatmeal was his favorite breakfast. "Well, what about the birthday parties this weekend?" Martin asked. "I hope everyone shows up. Have you heard from Chris and Jennifer?"

Susan gave Martin a curious look. "I think everything will turn out fine." She checked her watch again. "Okay, guys, time to hit the road. You don't want to be late."

CHAPTER THREE

May 4, 2020, 9:00 a.m.

You can do this, Martin. You have to.

He paused near the entrance to the office, a red wooden door that might have belonged to an old Colonial-home had it not been so large. Luke had been silent during the drive, but he'd jumped from the car and bravely walked across the parking lot. There had been a slight hesitation in his step, though—something only a father might notice—and Martin could sense the tension building.

"Your mother mentioned that she wants to go out to eat tonight. She wants you to pick the restaurant."

His attempt to calm Luke wasn't working. Martin was nervous, too, and Luke could tell. He tried again. "Maybe we can go to that pizza place you like, the one with all the video games."

Luke didn't answer. He grabbed the door and pushed it open.

Martin followed before Luke could change his mind.

The receptionist, a neatly dressed young man sitting inside a walled-off area with window-like openings, shuffled some papers on his desk and came to one of the windows. "You must be Luke?"

"I ready," Luke said, his voice edgy and a bit too loud.

Martin just stood there with his legs locked into place. He should have been thinking ahead, ready for whatever situation that might arise, but everything about this office suddenly seemed out of place.

The receptionist maintained his calm facade. He was probably used to dealing with uneasy clients.

"You must be Mr. Taylor," the receptionist said, "Luke's father?"

All Martin could manage to do was nod like some bobble-headed doll. "That's right." Martin put his arm around Luke's shoulder, but Luke tensed and stepped back. It was a reaction he seldom gave, and it was not a good sign.

"Sorry," Martin said. "We're both a little rattled this morning."

The receptionist gathered some papers and fastened them to a clipboard. "You'll need to fill this out. Both sides, please."

Martin took the clipboard and walked to an area where a row of chairs lined the wall, and Luke followed. So far, so good. He thought about telling Luke that everything would be all right, that it wouldn't take long, but decided against it. Best not to push it. Anyway, he had an uneasy feeling in his stomach, and he wasn't at all sure everything *would* be all right.

A few minutes later, Martin handed the clipboard to Luke and pointed to an underlined area where his son was to sign the document.

Luke took the clipboard and pen. He brought the pen to the paper as if to comply, but then he paused.

Before Martin could figure out what was happening, Luke hurled the clipboard onto the floor and stormed out of the office.

The other patients drilled Martin, an obviously bad father, with angry stares.

"Maybe you should go after him," one of them said.

Martin didn't know what to say, much less what to do about the situation. He sat there stunned, staring at the door that had closed behind his son. It might not have been the worst thing that could have happened, but it was close. An image of Luke stalking away, perhaps even walking into traffic, ran through Martin's mind, and the frightening truth of his lack of parenting skills put a knot in his stomach. Sitting there looking helpless might be taken by the others in the office as a sign of weakness.

He stood to go after Luke, steadying himself on legs that felt like rubber. He had to do something.

Thankfully, Luke resolved the issue. The door opened, and he came back into the office. He paused before strolling back to the chairs along the wall and lowered himself into a chair. "I sorry."

Martin smiled and sat back down. "It's okay, nothing to be sorry about. It took a lot of courage to come back in here like that. I'm proud of you."

Luke picked up the clipboard and then scooped up the pen. After signing the paperwork, he handed it to Martin.

"I'll take that," the receptionist said. "Doctor Stewart is ready. You'll need to wait here, Mr. Taylor. It's Doctor Stewart's policy to visit one-on-one with the patient. I hope you understand."

Martin nodded, but he wasn't so sure he did understand. He always went in with Luke on doctor's visits; his presence benefitted both parties. No one had ever objected before.

"It okay," Luke said. He followed the nurse, or whatever she was, out of the reception area. They both disappeared as the door, a freshly painted white door, closed behind them.

An uneasy sensation crept through Martin. He couldn't shake the feeling that he'd let Luke down, that he lacked the courage to do anything and had let his son walk alone into a situation that, for Luke, was scary and possibly even unsafe.

Martin pushed the ridiculous notion aside and leaned back into his chair, trying to relax, but his thoughts rambled. Writing was one of his passions, not that he'd had any real success with it. But he loved it, so he kept at it. Characters and scenes often ran through his mind. He'd found he could think of writing on the inside while carrying on with reality on the outside. But this was different. His characters and situations had always been fictional until now.

Now, he thought of Susan.

●　　●　　●

While Susan drove, Martin sat gazing through the passenger's side window, clinching his jaw.

"Martin Taylor, what in blazes is wrong with you?"

"Let me explain."

"Well, it had better be good. One simple task, Martin, that's all I asked. Take Luke to an appointment. And what do you do? Get into a fight with the doctor. Are you freaking kidding me?"

Susan paused. Tears moistened her eyes. "This is important, Martin. Luke's insurance coverage rests on it. Or doesn't that matter to you? I'm beginning to wonder if anything matters to you anymore. What were you thinking? You've never said a harsh word to anyone that I know of and now you're punching out doctors. I haven't seen the inside of a jail before, much less bail anyone out. I don't even know you anymore."

"Doctor Stewart was out of line, spouting off insulting statements about Luke's intelligence."

Susan went silent for a moment, as if she was trying to take in what Martin had said.

His hand balled into a fist, and he forced himself to calm down. He and Susan had gone through things like this before, too many times to count. It wasn't easy raising someone like Luke. But it had strengthened them— brought them all closer as a family.

"It was a psychological exam, Martin. The doctor had to make some determinations. I know these problems are too close to the surface for both of us. But maybe the doctor was just being...well, just being blunt about the matter."

"I might believe that," Martin said, "if I had been the one Doctor Stewart had spoken to about it."

"What are you saying?"

"That I heard it from Luke."

Susan frowned. "That makes it even worse. You know perfectly well how Luke gets things mixed up. He could have completely misunderstood."

"You're missing the point. Why would a psychologist confide things of that nature to the patient, knowing full well he wouldn't understand?"

After a moment of silence, Susan said, "What exactly did the doctor tell him?"

"That you and I, his parents, didn't deserve this, and we'd be better off without him."

Susan slowed the car for a moment and then resumed some speed. "That doesn't make sense. Why would a doctor jeopardize his career like that?"

• • •

"Mr. Taylor?"

Martin shook off the reverie or whatever it was—a memory, a premonition—and then stood and strolled across the floor toward the reception area. Once there, he said, "May 4, 2003."

"What's that?"

"Luke's date of birth."

The neatly dressed young man smiled. "You've done this before."

Martin nodded, but he thought it odd that the receptionist should put it that way. "More than a few times," he said. "Seventy-two zero five South Mulberry Avenue."

The office door opened, and Luke came out. He lowered his gaze to the floor and walked to where Martin stood.

"Hey, buddy. How did it go? Not so bad, I'll bet."

"I don't know. Okay, I guess."

"You guys are good to go," the receptionist said. "Doctor Stewart will relay his findings to Luke's primary care physician."

Martin thought of asking why it would be handled that way but decided it was best to leave it for now and just get Luke out of the environment. At home, he would talk to Susan about it and go from there. "Thanks for your help," he said.

He strolled across the floor with Luke close behind. Then, his mind busy with thought, he pushed the door open with a shaking hand. Just as he stepped through the doorway, he couldn't resist an urge to glance back. It was then that he saw who he suspected was Doctor Stewart. For a brief moment, Martin looked into the doctor's eyes. A flash of something like familiarity filtered through his mind, only to disappear as quickly as it had come.

Martin thought about Luke's life. He'd been examined and questioned by doctors, who constantly told him that everything would be all right, when in fact it was far from that. At least, it must seem that way to Luke.

Concern ran through Martin. He got into his Audi, waited for Luke to get fastened up, and drove out of the parking lot.

Luke sat silently for a while. Then he said, "Can hummingbirds get sick? You know, eat too much?"

"I don't think so," Martin said. He'd recently hung some feeders, and Luke had become fascinated with the birds. Oddly enough, he referred to them as tiny flying horses. "They need a lot of energy."

"I thought they could get sick."

Luke had become intrigued with an old sign of Pegasus, the mythical flying horse, at an antique shop. Martin had bought it, though he'd paid too much for it, and Luke had asked for it to be hung on the wall over his bed. "Not really," Martin said. "God made them that way. Their wings move fast, so they need energy. They get it from nectar." He paused. "And from the sugar water we put out for them."

"I thought they could get sick."

"No, they burn it off."

"Kind of like you and Mom?"

Luke's insight was often remarkable. Then again, when he got into these circular thought patterns, he might simply say things that only seemed that way. "Sort of," Martin said. "Hummingbirds need energy to fly, so they fly to get energy. Mom and I want food to eat, a place to stay, and other nice things, and we have to work to get that. Like the birds, we work to live and live to work."

Luke grew silent again and stared through the passenger's window.

"Is everything all right?" Martin asked.

"You be happy without me?"

Martin gripped the steering wheel. He'd never gone beyond surprise with Luke. "Why would I ever be without you?"

"Some of my friends don't get to live at home."

Martin struggled to come to terms with what he was hearing. Earlier, at the Doctor's office, he'd gone through a scenario in which he and Susan discussed Doctor Stewart's improper behavior. But that had only been in his mind, hadn't it? "Did something happen with Doctor Stewart?"

Luke grew silent and looked through the window, but his behavior was enough of an answer.

Martin slowed the car. It was all he could do to maintain a reasonable amount of composure. "What did Doctor Stewart say?"

"You and Mom don't deserve this."

"He said that to you?"

"It's okay."

"No, Luke, it's not okay." Martin took the next exit and pulled off the highway.

"I don't want to go back."

"You don't have to. I promise. You can stay in the car while I talk to Doctor Stewart."

A few minutes later, Martin pulled into the parking lot where he and Luke had been earlier. He reached for the door, but Luke put a hand on his shoulder.

"The fence man took the orange cord, and a hummingbird flew past my ear. The man took the orange cord. I thought you gave it to him."

Martin leaned back and tried to relax. He and Susan were in the process of having a fence installed. It had been quite an ordeal, as they'd gone through several installers to get it done. "No," Martin said, "I didn't give it to him. He hasn't finished the job, anyway. Maybe he'll bring it back."

"There was a dove on the roof. The fence man's truck wouldn't start. He and that skinny guy pushed it down the driveway."

Martin opened the door. "We'll talk about it when I get back, okay?"

"No, Dad. Please don't."

Martin hesitated, once again going over the strange scenario in which Susan had scolded him for getting into a fight with Doctor Stewart. "Yeah," he said, "maybe you're right."

He closed the door and started the car. However, he'd gone only a few feet when he saw the black BMW parked near the rear of the building. Martin turned the steering wheel toward the black car and taxied toward it. In a spot just behind the BMW, he stopped and shut off the engine. The BMW appeared to be dent-free. If the car had been involved in an accident, it had already been repaired.

"What you do?" Luke asked.

Martin opened the storage compartment between the seats. His mother had always insisted he keep toothpicks in the car, God rest her soul, and the toothpicks were still there. Martin got one toothpick and then pushed the button that popped open the trunk. "Just a little insurance policy," he said.

Remembering the nightmare, Martin hastened to the trunk, withdrew a roll of duct tape, and headed toward the BMW. Stopping in an area in where he hoped he wouldn't be seen he glanced around. Then he removed the valve cover from the rear passenger-side tire of the BMW, and shoved the toothpick in until air started to come out and tapped it in place. During the task, a chill crawled up his spine. Doctor Stewart's eyes had frightened him because they were the same eyes he'd looked into just as the BMW crashed into his car. With that, a sensation of being watched came over him, and he imagined those cold, steely eyes now hovering over him.

"What you do?"

Martin jerked around, fully expecting he'd been caught letting the air out of Doctor Stewart's tires, but instead saw his son standing within a few feet of him. "Blast it, Luke! You just cost me several years of my life."

"What you mean?"

"Never mind," Martin said. "Let's get out of here."

They scrambled back into the Audi, and Martin drove, home.

After getting Luke settled in, he left his son at the house. Luke had shown that he was okay alone for short periods. In fact, it made him feel important—more grown up.

A few minutes later, Martin squeezed the steering wheel. Why was he so convinced that something nefarious was going on?

As he drove toward the office, each time he asked himself, he got the same answer. It was something he sensed, maybe even believed on some gut level. Conversely, why did everyone else, with the possible exception of Luke, seem so oblivious to what was obvious to Martin? Which brought up another important point. If he was convinced that Doctor Stewart was up to something wrong, what was he going to do about it? He wasn't exactly anyone's knight in shining armor. It wasn't that a single, devastating act had put him on such an unsteady course. It was the daily accumulation of subtle insults levied by his insecure father.

At a stoplight less than three miles from his work, Martin reconsidered. He shouldn't go to the office today. Luke's appointment had taken only a couple hours, as was expected, and he could still get in four or five hours. But with the unsettling thoughts about the dream and the appointment, he'd be useless. He hadn't discussed the appointment with Susan. He and Luke had decided—Luke, because he didn't want to deal with it anymore, and Martin, because he wasn't ready—that they would keep what happened after the doctor's appointment between themselves. Martin wasn't in the habit of keeping secrets, especially not from Susan. He needed time to sort this out.

At a convenience store along the route, he pulled off the road and called in, telling his supervisor he was taking the day off. After that, he called Susan.

She answered on the second ring. "Martin?"

"Yeah, there's something we need to talk about. Some weird things happened after the appointment."

"You got it over with, Martin. That's what matters. Just let it go, okay? I'll talk to you later. I have a lot to do today."

Martin hesitated. Susan's busy agenda had reminded him of something. "I could pick up Candy's gift if you want."

"I've been meaning to ask you about that," Susan said. "Why did you ask about Chris and Jennifer? And who in the world is Candy?"

Martin tried to speak but no words came out. What was happening to him? Finally, the words came. "You know, Luke's friend. Her birthday is next week."

"Doesn't ring a bell, but Luke has a lot of friends. Yeah, go ahead if you want."

Martin's Stomach tightened. Candy Barnes wasn't just any friend. She and Luke were close—they had been for years. And her parents, Chris and Jennifer, were his and Susan's good friends. Parents of disadvantaged children tended to stick together. "Chris and Jennifer always throw a big party for Candy," Martin said. "You and I read the invitation. We talked about it. You wanted to get her one of those dolls she likes."

The phone went silent. For a moment, Martin thought he'd lost the connection, but then she spoke.

"Martin, Chris and Jennifer Barnes don't have any children that I know of, and I certainly don't know anyone named Candy. I haven't a clue of what's going on with you, but I'm getting concerned."

Susan paused and then continued, "We've both been under a lot of stress lately. Maybe you should take a few days off. We could take Luke and drive down to visit Krystal and Charles, maybe even go to Galveston. You have always loved the beach. It'll do you good."

"Maybe I'll do that," Martin said, but his mind was not on visiting or the ocean. Krystal was Luke's older sister. She'd recently married Charles Le Flore, a petroleum engineer from Houston. "We'll talk about it later, okay."

Martin glanced at the dashboard. "I love you, Susan."

"Love you, too. Talk to you later."

Martin let the phone slide from his hand. The similarities between the dream and the actual appointment were too great to write off. And now, this thing with Candy. Either Martin had completely lost his mind, or something was going on—something wrong—and he had to get to the bottom of it. He needed to talk to someone about it, and he had a pretty good idea of who that might be.

CHAPTER FOUR

May 4, 2020, 9:00 a.m.

At his home in Arlington, Virginia, John let his commitment to his country win out once again, and he carefully placed the small, wooden panel he was working with onto his workbench and set the glue gun beside it. He had discovered that building model airplanes released the tension he was forced to live with.

John's phone rang, and though he recognized the ringtone, he picked up the phone and verified the number visually. Sure enough, it was his old colleague, Andrew.

Exiting the room that he'd converted into a workshop, John started down the hallway. He brought the phone to his ear, switched on the light to his home office, and lowered himself into the leather chair behind the desk. "To what do I owe this interruption of my leisure?" he asked. "We both know you never call to talk about the weather or the state of my health. I'm retired, my old friend, and I'd like to keep it that way."

"It's nice to hear from you too," Andrew said. "Sorry to ruin your day."

"You haven't answered my question."

"We've detected another rift," Andrew said. "Probably a recent disruption, but it's too early to confirm that."

Thoughts of Sylvia blossomed in John's mind, but he pushed them away. Sylvia was gone. She had been for a long time. "I'm old beyond my years, Andrew. Too much travel. Traces of me have been scattered all over the spectrum. They're all quite real in their own way, a most unpleasant sensation, especially at night when I'm alone."

"You've always been alone, never known you to be any other way."

"That's a lie, and you know it. What details do you have?"

"As far as we can tell, the epicenter was somewhere around Tulsa, Oklahoma, centering around a twenty-five-year-old, mentally challenged female. My guess is she exists in a timeline that's not her own. You know how it goes."

"Yeah, and that's exactly why I shouldn't get involved. Do we have names?"

"Candy Barnes."

John wiped away a tear running down his cheek. Sylvia would still be with him if he hadn't accepted the last assignment. He often wondered how things might have turned out if he had not, but what did that give him? A lot of sleepless nights, that's what.

"John?"

"Yeah, I'm still here, but I don't know why. For heaven's sake, Andrew, get somebody else."

"We don't have anyone else. No one even comes close to your experience."

"And how long have you known this was eventually going to be a problem? Steps should have been taken. I can't do it forever. I won't."

"It's not that simple, and you know it. I don't like it either, but let's face it: you're somewhat unique."

In John's mind, no one could be *somewhat unique*. Either you were, or you were not. It really was that simple. The phrase was just Andrew's way of sidestepping the fact that he had once again backed himself into a corner. John leaned back into the chair and stared through the window overlooking his garden. He'd gotten pretty good at gardening, building models, and solving crossword puzzles. He would do anything to take his mind off his work, except nothing really did.

Let's not leave out the magic, John.

Yes, how could he forget about the magic? He'd also become accomplished in the art of stage magic, sleight of hand. All well and good, except he rarely had an audience.

It was all in the genetics, and John often reminded himself that his *somewhat unique* abilities were a gift, and all gifts were from God.

"Are you still there?" Andrew asked.

"Who else is involved? Someone was probably caring for the subject."

"Like I said, the details are pretty sketchy at this point. She lived with her parents, Chris and Jennifer Barnes, a retired couple. They seem like nice people. Unusual, if that term can be used in our business, for such a thing. When extraordinary things happen in an extraordinary world...I've got a bad feeling about this, John. I wouldn't blame you if you walked away from it. But I hope, for the sake of what's good, you won't."

John tightened his grip on his phone.

Good for whom?

"What's life like for the parents now? Any lingering memories, talking nonsense to neighbors, that sort of thing?"

"That's where you come in. If you'll cooperate, I'll set up the travel arrangements and take care of everything. Well, what do you say? Are you in?"

John gazed through the window again, paying particular attention to the tomatoes. There was nothing like homegrown tomatoes. With certain produce, most would be hard-pressed to tell the difference between fresh and store-bought, but not so with tomatoes. It had to do with the ripening process and certain sugars, which formed only under the right conditions, giving the fruit its distinctive flavor when allowed to mature naturally. By comparison, fruit picked too early to accommodate shipping and other marketing necessities seemed...well, like a cheap imitation.

A shiver ran through John at the thought of bouncing uncontrollably through an unknown number of fragmented parallels, all of which would be similar. They would be real, but for John the parallels would be imperfect, an imitation of his own reality. "Anybody else from the department involved in this?"

"No, it's all on you, that is, if you agree."

"Anything you're not telling me? I want it all, none of these need-to-know situations or any other political bull crap. I suspect I'm in a position to demand such conditions. The minute I suspect anything like that, I'll drop the case immediately. Do we understand each other?"

"Are we getting crusty in our old age?"

John remained silent. After all, he hadn't truly decided to accept the assignment, and he just might not if things weren't handled to his liking.

"All right, John. You're a smart guy, and you've probably already guessed as much, but we have to investigate these folks."

"I think the term you mean is *interview*," John said, "a process much more involved than an investigation."

"Like I said, you're a smart guy. Come on, John. I'm just as concerned as you are about this. I know you don't believe that, but it's the truth. Tell me that you're in, that you'll help us out with this."

"I can't promise anything, but I'll give it some serious thought. I'll get back to you. That much I promise."

John ended the call and studied a photo of Sylvia hanging on his office wall. The photo shouldn't exist, but he'd had it professionally drawn, created by an artist who specialized in such things. It didn't look like a drawing. It looked quite real. If not for the aberrant rift he'd set in motion, he and Sylvia would still be together, celebrating their fifth wedding anniversary next month.

You're somewhat unique, John.

It was true. His fear of causing more harm, both to himself and to others, bordered on being an actual phobia, but what was he to do? With all the government's resources, he was still the only reliable traveler they had.

John had created his current situation, living in a universe where Sylvia Stewart did not exist. The trouble was, he was helpless to do anything about it.

It had been, relatively speaking, a routine assignment. A rift had been created, threatening the original timeline, his timeline, and the only way to stop it had been to go back and redirect the actions that had spawned the errant fragment.

Afterward, a quick investigation had revealed that Sylvia was a product of the fragment. Upon correcting the rift, he had lost the only love he'd ever known.

He had no family, one reason the department had chosen him, and he had slowly lost contact with friends. His entire social life now consisted of himself, unless one counted model airplanes and tomato plants as companions. He would take the assignment.

Three hours later, in the early afternoon, everything was arranged, when John showed up at the home of Chris and Jennifer Barnes. Andrew had told the old couple that John would be there to discuss insurance matters. It seemed an unlikely tactic to John, but he went with it. He suspected a team of shadowy department people were working behind the scenes, doing whatever it was they did on such occasions.

For John, though, a single nagging thought hung in the air: *Where do I go from here?*

John introduced himself to Mr. and Mrs. Barnes and then said, "I need to talk to you alone concerning these matters. It's important we aren't disturbed during the consultation."

"Not a problem," Chris said. "We were told it was important and made arrangements not to be bothered for a few hours. Everything should be good to go."

Again, John wondered if the department had access to mind-control technology that worked over the phone. He glanced around the house and then said, "We can sit around the dining room table, if that will work for you."

"That will be fine," Jennifer said. "I'll get us some coffee. Do you like yours black, Mr. Rainbow?"

The surname *Rainbow* was a ridiculous alias, but everyone always seemed to buy it at face value. "Cream and sugar would be nice."

John understood he had to connect with the old couple on a deep level, which would involve his practiced method. He watched Mrs. Barnes place the coffee cups on the table. When she sat down, he rose from his chair. "I have a few unorthodox ways of doing what I do," he said. "Please don't let it distract you." He strolled over to Mr. Barnes. "To assure you of my honest intentions, let me again shake your hand."

As Chris Barnes complied, John used a sleight-of-hand method—one he'd long ago discovered he was quite good at— and dropped a small pill into the man's coffee. He repeated the process with Mrs. Barnes and returned to his chair.

The drug, which put the subject into a sort of hypnotic state of mind, was fast acting and overly effective. "I think we are ready to begin," he said.

Mr. and Mrs. Barnes nodded.

"I need to ask you some questions," John said, "some of which might be of a personal nature. It's extremely important that you answer them as honestly as possible. Do you understand?"

The old couple nodded.

"That's good, very good indeed. First off, do you have any children?"

In unison, they slowly shook their heads.

"Are you absolutely sure about that? Do you have any memories, dreams, or plans that didn't work out, that sort of thing?"

Again, they shook their heads.

"Do you have relatives, brothers and sisters, moms and dads, aunts, uncles?"

They gave out the information, but it offered nothing that would explain their missing daughter. None of the relatives were named Candy or anything close.

"This one is important, so I will ask again. Have you experienced any strange dreams, any déjà vu moments, unusual thoughts?"

Once again, nothing relevant came from the inquiry, so John changed tactics. "Have you experienced any changes in routine or diet, or had any recent, unusual doctor's visits?"

John wasn't sure where the last question had come from, but he let it hang, hoping it might have been premonitory.

Mr. and Mrs. Barnes turned toward each other and nodded. "There was that doctor," Jennifer said. "What was his name, dear?"

John sat forward with piqued interest. "What sort of doctor, a general practitioner or a specialist?"

"He was a psychologist," Mrs. Barnes said.

"And why would either of you be seeing a psychologist?"

As if asked a question that made no sense, Mr. and Mrs. Barnes sat motionless and expressionless.

John pulled a small pad from his pocket and jotted down a few notes. "If you recall anything else about this doctor, let me know."

They nodded and then Mr. Barnes said, "For the life of me, I don't know what you are talking about, Jennifer. Why would you bring something like that up? We don't know any psychologists."

"Oh, we do," she said. "We've just forgotten."

"That's okay. You're doing fine. However, if you could remember the psychologist's name, that information would help me with my investigation."

Mrs. Barnes wrinkled her forehead in thought and then said, "The more I think about it, the more distant it gets."

"Kind of like a dream," Mr. Barnes said.

"Yes, dear, much like a dream."

John sat quietly for a moment and considered the situation. For the time being, Chris and Jennifer Barnes were aware of his presence on some level but oblivious to the true nature of the visit and unaware of his physical movements. Much like being under deep hypnosis, they could hear his voice and respond to his questions to the best of their ability. But for all practical purposes, he was like a ghost, free to roam about the grounds undisturbed, provided no friends, neighbors, or relatives showed up. The visit reinforced his earlier assumptions, and therefore, he couldn't imagine either of them having had anything to do with the past events.

"I'm going to have a look around, if you don't mind. Please sit quietly until I return. I promise I won't be long."

Chris and Jennifer Barnes nodded in unison.

Sadness ran through John. They seemed like nice, ordinary people. The question was, who caused this and why? What motivation could anyone have to risk causing so much potential damage?

"I understand what you're going through," he said, "even though you don't seem to at the moment. I will do my best to find out who has been meddling in your affairs and will do everything in my power to stop him."

John *Rainbow* then made a thorough search of the house and the attached garage. There were no other buildings on the property. He found nothing of interest, no equipment capable of causing a hole or a rip in time and no materials that could construct such machinery. He returned to the dining area, where Mr. and Mrs. Barnes sat quietly, their hands folded together in front of them.

"A few more questions," John said. After all, he had to be thorough. "Do either of you have any knowledge of or even a vague interest in the concept of time travel?"

They shook their heads.

"Do you know anyone who does?"

Again, they shook their heads.

This time, however, a slight hesitation preceded the action. "To the best of your knowledge, have you answered my questions correctly and truthfully? Search your memory to be sure."

"Yes, sir," they both answered, "the truth as we know it."

John thought the answer odd, though under the circumstances, it was nothing to note. However, the hesitation they'd displayed in answering the second to the last question concerned him. Any parallel or fragmented memories could be trouble.

He made one more pass through the house, paying particular attention to the bedrooms. The master was as it should be, and the second, spartan, with only a bed and a nightstand. But the third bedroom, the farthest from the master, was troubling. It was completely empty. Who kept a completely empty bedroom in their house? That, however, was not a perfect description. The bedroom was not completely empty. He bent down and scooped up an old envelope from the floor.

Once again, he returned to the area where Chris and Jennifer Barnes patiently waited. "I'm going to set the timer on your microwave oven," he said. "When it sounds, you will wake up refreshed and feeling well. Do you understand?"

They nodded.

"You will not remember my questions. You will not remember me. And you will have absolutely no memory of my having been here. Is that clear?"

The couple nodded.

With that, John left the house, locking the door behind him. More answers were to be found here, but he would not find them today.

Sitting in his car outside Chris and Jennifer Barnes' house, John opened the envelope he'd found in the third bedroom. It turned out to be an invitation to a birthday party—a party for Candy Barnes, interestingly enough.

CHAPTER FIVE

May 4, 2020, 12:30 p.m.

Martin angled off the road and pulled onto the asphalt drive, stopping at a locked, farm gate made of tubular steel and corrugated strips of metal. About three hundred yards beyond the gate, sat a double-wide trailer that Tanner McIntosh had dragged onto the property—a semi-wooded, two-acre lot a few miles east of town.

Martin had met Tanner during a church event, a day of service, painting houses. That now seemed an unlikely place to have met the man, and Martin wondered, as he had from the start, if coming here was a good idea. He and Tanner had little in common, but as soon as Martin had become convinced that Susan was being completely honest about not knowing Candy Barnes, he'd thought of Tanner. After all, he was Candy's uncle. Not only that, but he shared Martin's interest in the unusual. He and Martin had talked about such things during the house painting, and again at one of Candy's parties.

Martin didn't sound the horn. If Tanner wanted the visit, he'd show up shortly. If not, Martin would back out and go on his way. He'd called ahead, but Tanner hadn't answered. He seldom did.

Several seconds later, the gate swung open, and Martin guided the Audi along the winding drive toward the double-wide, which sat at the high point of the property. The gate's automation was something new. He pulled up in front of the fourth bay door of the garage—a large metal building that Tanner had built after moving onto the property. The garage looked newer than the house.

Martin sat for a moment. Then he climbed out of the Audi and leaned against the car, arms folded in front of him. Tanner made no sign indicating he even knew Martin was there. But Martin figured that he did. Someone had to have opened the gate.

Just inside the first bay door, Tanner worked on an old Harley-Davidson. A large pit bull terrier, something else that was different, sauntered over and sniffed Martin's leg.

"Becker, leave the man alone."

Martin loved animals, but pit bulls made him nervous. They always had. He suspected that the dog could sense his fear, which only made things worse. "Hello, Becker I came to talk to the boss. Is he available?"

The dog made no indication that he'd heard the greeting. He just stood there between Martin, and Tanner, his eyes locked on Martin's every move.

Keeping half of his attention on the dog, Martin turned toward the garage. "Hey, Tanner. What's up?"

"You're the one with the troubled look on your face. You tell me."

Martin had just put himself on the spot. He wished he were more decisive, more like Tanner. But he wasn't. He probably never would be. He didn't even know why he was there. But since he was, and he didn't know who else to turn to, he came out with it. "I'm not sure where to start," he said. "Things seem to be happening, weird things."

"Like what?"

Martin glanced at the dog and then back to the garage. It might be best to ease into it. "I've been having some troubling déjà-vu moments. Thought maybe you could help me sort it out."

Tanner got to his feet, wiped his hands with an oil rag, and then retrieved something from his pocket and pulled his hair back into a ponytail. He sauntered over to where Martin was standing. Then, like some misplaced cowboy, he leaned into the car, bringing his face within inches of Martin's.

He'd always reminded Martin of Sam Elliot, except this version had more tattoos and seemed rougher around the edges, if that were possible.

"You came all the way out here to talk about something as benign as that?" Tanner pushed away from the car and then walked away, strolling across the yard. He didn't ask Martin to follow.

If Tanner's expression meant anything, Martin suspected he'd be better off getting back in his car and driving away, but he wouldn't do that. Something kept him there, and whatever it was it was overcame his fear of both Tanner and the dog.

Martin found Tanner about fifty yards from the garage, sitting in a lawn chair. Tanner had constructed a crude patio made of pavers. He'd fashioned a barbecue out of a thirty-gallon drum and placed a couple of wooden lawn chairs beside the cooker. Between the chairs, a metal ice chest that looked antique enough to be a decorator piece sat on a wooden pallet.

"What's this all about, Martin? Having a little fun with me because I'm a little out there? If you have a problem outside the ordinary, from Bigfoot to UFO's, then Tanner's your man, right?"

Martin sat down in the other lawn chair. He'd never seen this side of Tanner, and discovering that the guy he secretly looked up to wasn't as tough as he seemed didn't help. "It's nothing like that," he said. "Things that I don't understand are happening. I'm afraid, Tanner. I thought maybe you could help. That's all."

Tanner smirked. "Now what in blazes could the stoic Martin Taylor be afraid of?"

Martin sat forward. He'd thought of himself in many different ways. Half of his mental energy was spent worrying about what other people thought of him, but he'd never considered himself stoic. What's more, he was compelled to lay it all out, as if Tanner were some high-powered psychologist or something.

"Everything, Tanner. God only knows what I go through. But that's another story. This time, I think I have myself a real problem."

"All right, then. What's this all about?"

"Susan woke me up this morning, telling me I was going to be late for an appointment. Trouble is, she brought me out of a dream that was pretty much the same thing I was supposed to be late for."

Tanner reached into the ice chest, pulled out a can, and popped it open. "Beer?" he asked.

Martin considered it but shook his head. "I still have to drive home."

Tanner took a swig. "Dreams are one thing, and déjà-vu is another. At any rate, there's a mountain of information out there. Anybody who wants to can find it with a little Internet browsing. Of course, like everything else, ninety-nine percent of it is garbage. Then again, if you can locate some common threads, sometimes you can get the gist of what's valid and what's not."

Martin hesitated and then decided he'd already gone this far; there was no sense in holding back. "What do you know about time travel?"

Tanner leaned back in his chair and sipped his beer. Moments later, he said, "Could you tell me a little more about this dream?"

Martin shifted in his chair, trying to get comfortable. He then relayed everything to Tanner as best he remembered it, including the doctor's visit, the accident, and the discovery that he and Luke had yet to make the appointment.

Afterward, Tanner stared into space for what seemed a long time.

An uneasy feeling crept through Martin, and he considered changing the subject, or passing it off as an effort at conversation. He could not bring himself to do that. "So, what do you think?"

Tanner studied Martin's face. "When was the appointment?" he asked.

Martin shrugged. "It was today."

"And you went to it, you and Luke?"

"That's right. We got out of there around 10:30 a.m. After dropping Luke off, I came straight here."

"And what about Doctor Stewart and his car?"

"It all happened just like I told you." He paused before adding, "At least from my perspective."

Tanner narrowed his eyes, which caused lines to form across his forehead. "Then I guess we should pray that you are delusional, and that what you thought you experienced was, in fact, some kind of unusual, lucid dream."

Martin was not sure he should ask the next question, but it came out anyway. "And what if it was real and not a dream?"

"If, in fact, you've already lived this entire day and are now taking a second stab at it, then I'd say we have a real problem on our hands."

Martin had consumed no alcohol in at least five years. He had never been a heavy drinker; he ordered a drink only occasionally when he and Susan went to dinner. But alcohol was one thing he'd given up when he accepted Jesus into his life. However, Pastor Meadows had once said the alcohol itself wasn't the sin, but rather the abuse of it. Martin didn't think having a drink now with Tanner would constitute abuse.

"Is that beer offer still open?" he asked.

"Help yourself."

Martin fished a can from the ice and popped it open. "Why would that be a problem?"

"You're kidding me, right? Tell me, on the first go-around, did you and I have this little visit?"

"No," Martin said. "We didn't."

Tanner shook his head. "If it's even possible, and I don't know that it is, do you have any idea of the consequences of your actions, of what you might have set in motion?"

"I guess I kind of thought there might be some repercussions."

"Repercussions? Martin, going on the assumption that this is real, you've altered your timeline and, in addition, anybody else's you might have come into contact with today. There's no telling what you've done."

Martin leaned back in the chair. He did not know what else to say, much less how to offer any such revelation.

"You're a good man," Tanner continued, "and the best father Luke could hope for, but let's face it. You worry like someone's grandmother. I'm sure you were all keyed up and went to bed, fretting over the possibility of Luke getting unruly or even uncooperative during the appointment. It's no wonder you had a nightmare. Concentrate on the dream. Is there anything else you can remember about it?"

Martin closed his eyes and let his thoughts roam free for a moment. When he reopened them, he said, "Does the term *Camp Hero* mean anything to you?"

Tanner's face lost a couple shades of color. "It's a name associated with the Air Force base in Montauk, New York. Question is, how do you know about it?"

Martin shrugged. "It was part of the dream. There were voices. One of them might have said something like that. But they were in the background, more like whispers. It's probably nothing."

An expression somewhere between fear and excitement ran across Tanner's face. "I don't know about that," he said. "It just might be the most substantive thing you've told me today."

Martin wanted to press forward, ask about Candy, but decided against it. He opted for a momentary distraction to ease the mood. "I noticed the old Harley in the garage. What do you have going on with that?"

"Not just any old Harley," Tanner said, "a 1947 Knucklehead, kind of rare and pretty pricey. Guy that owns it is supposed to pick it up today." He paused and shrugged. "It keeps me busy. Pick up a few dollars now and then. How about you? Do you ride?"

"Yeah, it's been a few years. Had a couple of scooters when I was a kid, and later, in college, rode a 350 but I've never tried anything like a Harley."

Tanner smiled, the first time he'd shown any lightheartedness. "We need to get you on a Harley. Might loosen some of that tension between your ears."

"Yeah," Martin said, "I'd like that." He paused. "On the level, Tanner, this time-travel thing, do you believe it's possible?"

"Well, it's kind of like this. I love thinking about stuff like that, reading it, watching it on TV, but actually believing it—I don't know if I'm ready to take that step or not."

At any other time, Martin would have been relieved by that. But this wasn't any other time. "I wish I could say the same. You mentioned earlier that reliving today, or any other past event, could alter the timeline—change things—and not all for the good."

"What exactly are you getting at?"

"Changes," Martin said, "differences in the way things were before."

"Like what, for example?"

Martin glanced eastward to an area where an aging tractor sat, a trailer of some kind attached to the hitch. "You have some new motorcycles, a few more tattoos, a dog, and there used to be some playground equipment where the tractor is."

Tanner grinned. "Interesting, but not exactly earth-shattering news, is it? At least a month has passed since you were here before. None of it's real, mind you, but even if it were, it's easily explainable given the amount of time that's passed."

Martin nodded. Time to bring out the big guns. "The playground equipment was for Candy Barnes, your niece and Chris and Jennifer's daughter."

Tanner rose from the lawn chair and walked over, all six foot two inches of him hovering above Martin.

For a moment, Martin thought the old biker might just drag him from the chair and give him a beating, but Tanner turned and started back toward the garage.

"I guess I should go," Martin said. "I didn't mean to upset you." That much was true. He had wanted to get Tanner's attention. That's all. He'd done that, though maybe not in the most productive way. He got up from the chair, but instead of leaving, he followed Tanner into the garage.

Several bikes in various stages of restoration were arranged across the center part of the area. Along the north wall, five fully assembled Harleys were lined up and ready. Martin had once again gained the attention of the pit bull. The dog got up from his sleeping position, padded over, and stared up at Martin, his canine face expressionless. A bead of sweat slipped down from Martin's arm pit. If the dog lunged, would Tanner, care?

"I'm sorry," Martin said. "It's just that things are happening that I don't understand. I'm sorry I bothered you." Martin turned to leave, but he had only taken a few steps when Tanner spoke.

"Not so fast. We haven't finished our business."

Martin turned back. After all, Tanner controlled the gate that would let him out. "What do you mean?"

He swept his hand toward the bikes. "It's time for that riding lesson, my friend."

"I don't know," Martin said. "It's been a long time, and I've never ridden a bike that big. Maybe some other time."

"I'm afraid I have to insist," Tanner said. "There's nothing to worry about. It's like falling off a horse. Once you've done it, you never forget."

He rolled a bike out and onto the drive. "Anyway, it's a small one, an XLCH, only 900cc. You should be able to handle it, seeing as you rode a 350. Climb on, and I'll show you the gear pattern and where the brakes are. After that, it's just a matter of getting your confidence up."

With a glance, Martin considered Becker, who was still staring at him, and then looked back to Tanner. Martin had a habit of taking the path of least resistance. Susan reminded him of the fault often enough. He just tried to avoid trouble, that's all. The best choice with this problem, though, was to go along with it—get on the Harley and make it happen. Maybe the ride would lighten the mood, take a little of the edge off. "All right," he said. "What the heck? It should be fun." He climbed onto the Harley. "I just hope I don't crash into anything."

"Better not," Tanner said. "Becker likes that one. He watched me the whole time while I was working on it. I don't know why. Dogs seem to have their own little world, don't they?" After firing up his bike, Tanner eased it onto the driveway, heading toward the exit.

Martin started his bike, then struggled to keep it steady as he pulled onto the driveway. As he and Tanner neared the gate, it swung open. Tanner must have brought a remote with him.

At the main road, Tanner motioned forward and headed west.

They didn't talk. Tanner just drove, and Martin followed.

About thirty or forty minutes later, Tanner pulled off of 11th Street, and Martin followed him through the gates of Oak Lawn Cemetery.

They paused at the stone structure near the entrance, but no one came out. It was the middle of the day in the heart of Midtown Tulsa, a bustling area by Oklahoma standards. However, the cemetery did not share the same level of activity. To Martin, the place had an almost abandoned feel to it, an island of desolation avoided even by the down-and-out and homeless.

Tanner shut off his bike and put it on the stand. Then, he climbed off and started walking along a pathway leading to the gravesites.

Martin had a bad feeling about the whole thing, but he shut down his bike and followed.

About halfway down the lane, Tanner stepped off the pathway and walked several feet before stopping. "Here," he said, pointing to a headstone. "This is what I want you to see."

Martin trudged over to where Tanner was standing and glanced down at the Marble headstone, carved into the shape of a lamb. It was obvious someone had made an occasional stab at keeping the grounds clean but to Martin the cemetery looked as if it hadn't been mowed in a few weeks. Even then, it was only mowed, no trim work. Most of the headstones were just partially visible because weeds surrounded them.

Tanner reached down, grabbed a fist full of weeds, and ripped them away from the headstone. "Read it," he said.

Martin already strongly suspected what he was about to see, but he forced himself to look anyway. It read: Candy Lynne Barnes, May 15, 1995— May 19, 1995.

"We never talk about this," Tanner said, "neither I nor Chris, nor Jennifer." He paused, veins bulging slightly along his forehead. "I don't know how you found out, Martin, or why you would do such a thing, but it ends here. Understand? If I ever hear of you going to Chris or Jennifer about this, it won't be good for you. I guarantee it. Do you understand?"

"Yes," Martin said, "but I didn't go looking for this, any of it. It came looking for me. I know about Candy because I have known her a long time. She and Luke were friends. They even worked together for a while. Susan and I went with Luke every year to her birthday party. Sometimes the party was held at your place. Candy and Luke played on the playground equipment you had there. This is real, Tanner. It's real, and it's happening. I don't have the slightest idea of how to deal with something like this. That's why I came to you. I need your help."

"It's a little outside my wheelhouse, old buddy. There's only so much a good Harley can do. You need help all right. You need a good shrink."

"A shrink is the last thing I need. As far as I can tell, this all started with Doctor Stewart. He tried to take Luke and me out on the highway. I think he'll try again. It's not about me, though. It's all about Luke. I don't know how I know that, but I do. Luke's in danger, and it looks like I'm the only one standing between him and another altered timeline."

"I hate to say it now," Tanner said, "seeing what a mixed-up bundle of nerves you are, but I'm totally confused by all of this and still undecided whether you're being straight or playing me for a fool. I always looked up to you, Martin. Thought you had it more together than most." He shook his head. Then he turned away and started back toward the roadway. "Some role model you turned out to be."

Martin gathered his thoughts. How could it be that someone like Tanner McIntosh could admire Martin Taylor, a man who went out of his way to avoid conflict?

Martin bowed his head at the gravesite of Candy Barnes and offered a silent prayer for her soul, wherever it might be. Then, he prayed for himself, Luke, and anyone else who was caught up in this mess. After finishing the prayer, he walked across the cemetery grounds and back to the roadway.

Tanner was already sitting on his Harley, staring at the exit, his face expressionless.

"Humor me for a moment," Martin said.

Tanner didn't reply or break his silent stare, but he didn't start his bike and leave either.

"Suspend your disbelief," Martin continued, "and pretend I'm not crazy. If I were, in fact, caught up in some kind of time rift, how could I fix it? What could I do to put things back the way they were?"

Tanner shook his head. "I don't know that you could. If what you read about the subject is to be believed, anything you did would only make things worse, create more fractures or splinters or whatever."

Martin climbed onto his bike and stared ahead without speaking. However, the silence and desolation of the cemetery soon overwhelmed him. "I can't just let it go," he said. "Something is going on, Tanner, something bad. I don't know why I'm the only one who seems to see it. I wish to God it wasn't like that. But knowing what I know, that things have changed, and not all of it for the better"—he paused, the weight of what he was saying crashing in on him— "we have to do something."

"I suppose," Tanner said, his voice strained, "that if you could figure out a way to go back, and I'm definitely not sure it's even possible or how you might pull it off if it were, but if you could—"he paused—"and this is just a theory, nothing scientific about it, but if you could determine the exact time and place where the original fracture occurred and go back there, right before it happened, you might be able to stop it. But everything, the people, the time, and the place would have to be exact."

"Then I need someone, someone to fix this, put things back the way they were."

"I don't know that anything needs to be fixed, my friend. Even if it did, I certainly don't have a time machine. And I don't know anybody who does."

With that, Tanner fired up his Harley and sped out of the cemetery.

Martin stayed behind, tried to gather his senses, though in the silence of the deserted cemetery, an unnerving sensation of being watched lingered. He glanced around, saw no one, and then started the bike and drove away. Being alone in a graveyard where people who shouldn't be dead were buried would do that to you. He mentally charted a course that would lead him back to Tanner's place. The old biker was completely out of sight by now, and he might not be heading home, but Martin didn't know what else to do.

CHAPTER SIX

May 5, 2020, 3:00 p.m.

John sat in his car in front of a two-story brick-and-frame house on Mulberry Avenue in Broken Arrow, a suburb of Tulsa. After the Barnes interview, he had gone back to his hotel room, where a few minutes of Internet research had given him the address to his present location.

He grabbed his phone and punched in the number, waiting until the other party answered.

"I've run across something rather disturbing," John said. "Thought you should know."

"I'm not surprised. I only wish I were."

"Yeah, well, at any rate, neither Chris nor Jennifer Barnes were responsible for the fracture."

"Are you sure?"

A curtain, covering a front window of the house moved, catching John's attention, and he hesitated. His presence there had been detected.

"Yes," he answered. Had there been any impressions of time travel, he would have sensed it. He was peculiar that way, according to Andrew. "I am."

"I'm not sure whether that revelation is encouraging or disappointing," Andrew said, "but I don't see it as disturbing."

"Mrs. Barnes rambled on about some doctor's appointment. It didn't seem to go anywhere. It's probably nothing."

"You're stalling, John. What are you trying to tell me?"

"A search of the Barnes' house turned up clean, except for one thing. In an otherwise empty bedroom, I found an anomalous invitation."

"An unusual choice of words," Andrew said. "Tell me more."

"It's an invitation to a birthday party for Candy Barnes. Since she doesn't exist in this timeline, neither should the invitation."

"You're right. That is disturbing."

"It gets worse. It's probably not an isolated incident. There could be multiple fractures."

"Why do I get the feeling you're still holding back?"

John glanced through the windshield. Several houses up, some children played in the yard, laughing and chasing one another. It was a beautiful neighborhood in suburban America, a life he had never known, apart from his short time with Sylvia.

"It's the perpetrator," he said. "I think it might be our mystery traveler."

For what seemed an inordinate amount of time, the phone transmitted only silence. When Andrew finally answered, his doubtful thoughts came through in his tone.

"Come on, John. Don't go to pieces on me now. I need you to see this through. We both know where your fear of traveling leads."

John held the steering wheel so hard he thought it might break under the pressure. The maddening thing about it was that a time disturbance created by an anonymous traveler a few years earlier had brought Sylvia into John's world. To the best of John and Andrew's knowledge, the traveler, either a legitimate doctor or someone posing as one, had gone back to cause the stillbirth of Angela Stewart—a possible, distant relative who would have been born with Down's Syndrome—which had caused the emergence of Sylvia. John's putting things back in their proper order brought Angela back, but eliminated Sylvia.

"Think about it, Andrew: Jennifer Barnes mentioning a doctor, the stillbirth of Angela Stewart, and the near same thing with Candy Barnes, who was also mentally challenged. I'm not going to pieces. I'm laying out the facts. This has the traveler's fingerprints all over it."

"You can't bring Sylvia back."

"Don't you think I realize that? You're the one who asked for my help. You tell me what you want me to do."

"All right, just don't get crazy on me. I need to give it some thought."

"While you're thinking, let me add to your worries. The anomalous invitation was addressed to someone."

"I'm almost afraid to ask."

"It was addressed to Luke, Susan, and Martin Taylor."

"And how, pray tell, are they connected?"

"I don't know the answer to that yet, but I'm parked on the street in front of their house."

"You're an amazing man, John. What do you intend to do?"

"I suppose an interview is in order."

"Do you want me to set it up?"

John studied the house. The gardens were well tended, the lawn neatly mowed. He would soon disrupt a family, something he did not want to do. Then again, he supposed they already had been disrupted, whether or not the participants knew.

"If that's what you want to do; however, I am here now. I could go in cold."

"I'm not sure I like the idea, but the way things have been going, it might be best to interview them while you have the chance. No time like the present, right?"

"You got it," John said. He ended the call. Unfortunately, Andrew's cheap pun had been intended. He sat for another moment or two. Then, he climbed out of the car and started toward the door.

CHAPTER SEVEN

May 4, 2020, 2:00 p.m.

As soon as Martin pulled onto the asphalt, the gate swung open, allowing him to glide down the driveway without having to slow his pace on the Harley.

Stopping in front of the first bay door, Martin swung off the bike and walked cautiously along the trail that had been beaten into the grass leading to the front door of the double-wide. To his relief, the dog was nowhere to be seen, though he found it disconcerting that Tanner was apparently in the house and not working in the garage. He didn't know why he had thought it might be that way, only he couldn't recall ever seeing the garage closed in the daytime. Then again, he hadn't been here that often.

The front door to the double-wide flew open a few steps before he reached it. Tanner was still upset.

Acting as if it were just another day in his life, Martin walked into the living room, then strolled across the floor to the counter separating the kitchen from the rest of the house, and placed the keys to the Harley on the bar. "Thanks for the ride," he said. "We'll have to do it again sometime."

Tanner acted as if he wanted to smash his fist into the wall. It seemed to Martin that such behavior was not uncommon for the old biker. Judging from the wall décor—the mismatched panels of sheet metal Martin had previously wondered about—repairs had been made to the walls more than once.

"Okay," Martin said, "I'm sorry about all of this. I never intended to upset you. And I completely understand why you would be. You probably think I'm crazy. Maybe you're right. Don't think that possibility hasn't crossed my mind."

Tanner plopped onto one of the barstools "You were just trying to get some help. Something you need all right, but I don't think it's the kind I can deliver." He popped open a beer. "Just look at me. How many times have I wished for something like this to be real? And now that it's been brought to my doorstep, what have I done? I've turned into the kind of critic I've always resented on TV—the stuffy professor who proclaims UFO sightings have been perpetuated by nothing more than errant weather balloons."

"I don't think I'm following you."

"It's probably best you don't. You're saying all of this started with some doctor's visit. Maybe you're overreacting, transferring some hidden fears onto a benign situation."

Tanner was vacillating all over the place. Martin couldn't tell if the man was on his side or not, and without warning, the whole thing angered him, an emotion he wasn't used to or comfortable with.

"It's not like that at all," he said. "Whether or not you believe it, this is happening." Martin should have stopped there. He knew that. He continued anyway. "This isn't the way things are supposed to be, Tanner. I know that just as sure as I'm standing here. Candy shouldn't be in the graveyard. And God only knows what else is wrong, what's been changed because of this."

"All right," Tanner said, "settle down. Tell you what, how about I have a little talk with this doctor?"

Again, Martin was caught off guard by Tanner's change in direction. "Why would you want to do that?"

"Your old buddy has a few tricks up his sleeve. I know how to deal with *those* kinds of doctors, how to make them think they are in control, handling me while I'm handling them. If he has even the slightest degree of shade on his mantle, I'll see through it. Trust me on this."

Martin wasn't sure what to think about that, but he believed Tanner just might deliver on such a promise. He couldn't let him do it, though. If Doctor

Stewart was up to something nefarious, there was no telling what Tanner might be getting himself into.

"That won't be necessary. Luke's already convinced me that something unusual went down during his appointment."

"Of course, you know Luke better than I do," Tanner said, "better than anyone, I'll bet, but sometimes it takes an outsider to point out what's not so clear to insiders."

Martin didn't like where this was going. "What are you getting at?"

"Just that Luke has more going for him than you give him credit for."

"And just how would you know that?"

"We've talked," Tanner said, "though I must admit, I can't remember when or where."

Martin nodded. The answer had occurred to him while Tanner was speaking. "I think I know," he said. "It was during the birthday parties you hosted for Candy. Luke loved your playground equipment just as much as she did."

An uneasy look crossed Tanner's face, just as a dog, somewhere outside the double-wide, began barking.

Tanner rose from the barstool and strolled toward the front door.

"What is it?" Martin asked.

"Becker's barking. Becker never barks."

Tanner flung open the door and stepped out.

Martin came out of the double-wide, but he'd taken only a few steps onto the grass when the first shot was fired. Not that Martin knew what it was at first. He did not. When a bullet hole formed, however, in the sheet metal not more than two feet from his head, he put it all together.

Tanner was screaming something, probably for Martin to get down. But Tanner was not obeying his own command.

Martin sensed what was going to happen, which ran a current of fear through him. It wouldn't do to tell the biker to get himself out of the line of fire. Martin would have to physically take him down.

Martin started toward Tanner, though it was like a dream in which his legs would not work properly. His muscles strained as if he were walking through thick mud. He struggled to make it through, but he began to lose concentration. He became dizzy, and everything went out of focus.

● ● ●

Martin opened his eyes to total darkness, though he immediately knew where he was. He felt the electricity along the narrow walls and heard the distant voices, as before. He was back in the tunnel, or whatever it was. Perhaps he had never left, and everything else was some kind of dream. He didn't believe that though. He detected something different this time: the smell of medicine.

He knew only one thing. He had to get back and save Tanner. He thought of an old-fashioned calendar. He wasn't sure why, but since he had the image in his mind, he concentrated on the fourth day of May. Taking it further, he brought the face of his grandfather's watch to mind and mentally adjusted the hands to 1:57 p.m.

● ● ●

A flash of blue light nearly blinded Martin. He tightened his grip on the handlebars of the Harley Davidson, but he did not pull immediately onto the asphalt driveway, leading to Tanner's place. Instead, he rode a few hundred yards south, where he pulled off the road as best as he could without going into the ditch. Almost as if acting on instinct, though on some level he understood what he was doing, he shut off the bike and started walking east along the fence line bordering Tanner's property. He'd made it about fifty feet when the leaves shuffled, and someone ran from the cover of trees. He couldn't see anyone, but he had a strong sensation that he'd accomplished, at least for the time being, what he'd set out to do.

Martin remounted the bike and drove toward the entrance to Tanner's property. He'd gone back in time, or something, and it had happened on the day that he suspected he was already doing over. A bead of sweat formed on his spine and trickled down his back. Why, was this happening? And why, of all people, was it happening to him?

Again, the gate swung open, and Martin guided the bike along the black asphalt driveway. Near the first bay door, he shut down the Harley. Then, he climbed off and started walking along the grassy pathway toward the entrance to the double-wide.

The door opened the way it had before just as he neared the entrance. As if following a script, Martin walked to the bar and placed the keys to the Harley on the counter.

Tanner stood near the doorway, leaning against the bar, a can of beer in his hand. "Hello, Martin. I wish I could say it was good to see you again."

For a moment, Martin considered the old biker's words. "What's the matter, Tanner? You look like you've seen a ghost?"

Tanner plopped onto a barstool. "Maybe I have, but the last time I checked, you were the one with the déjà-vu problem."

"Funny you should put it that way," Martin said. He walked to the window beside the front door, parted the mini blinds, and peeked out.

Becker was lounging peacefully in the flower bed beside the front steps.

Martin was relieved the dog was still there. Things had a way of changing in his world. He checked his grandfather's watch.

It showed 2:15 p.m., Monday, May 04. If bullets were going to fly, it should happen any minute now. Another frightening thought occurred to Martin. Earlier, at the cemetery, he'd thought someone was watching him, and less than an hour later, the sniper attack had unfolded. He thought of Luke and Susan. Where were they right now?

"I should go," he said. "I need to check on my family."

"Wait. That's not a good idea, not just yet."

Tanner knew. Martin had suspected it earlier. What makes you say that? Could it be a premonition that someone hiding in the trees will shoot at me as soon as I step outside?"

Tanner raised the beer to his lips, drained the contents, and then crushed the can with his hand. "Something like that," he said. He got up from the barstool and walked over, stopping a few feet away from Martin. "What in the hell have you done, Martin Taylor? What in the hell have you gotten us into?"

Martin shook his head. "I don't know that I've done anything."

That's not true, is it Martin? You just ran someone out of the trees and possibly stopped an ambush.

"I don't know what's going on, Tanner, and that's the truth."

What about the tunnel, Martin? How did you get there? And for that matter, how did you get back out of it?

"I don't know whether I'm causing this or if I'm just caught up in it. I'm sorry I dragged you into it."

Martin turned and reached for the door.

"Wait," Tanner said. "What if it happens again, the shooting I mean? You'll never make it to your car. And then what?"

Martin parted the mini blinds and peeked out. The dog was still there. "Becker's not barking."

"Becker never barks."

"But he's lying there as if everything is cool. He wouldn't do that if there was trouble, would he?"

Tanner shrugged. "Probably not, but I wouldn't stake my life on it."

"I have to," Martin said. "What if that maniac goes after Susan or Luke?"

Tanner rubbed his forehead. "I never would have guessed hanging around with mild-mannered Martin Taylor would add such suspense to my life. I can't let you go it alone, though. I guess we should ride over and check it out."

Martin opened the door and stepped onto the landing. Then he paused and scanned the area. He saw nothing out of the ordinary, heard nothing unusual. "You don't have to do this, Tanner. I wouldn't blame you at all if you walked away. And who knows, maybe this only happens around me, and maybe you would be just fine without me in the picture."

Tanner turned and disappeared into the double-wide. When he returned, he was carrying a large revolver.

"I'm knee-deep in this already," Tanner said. "I can't let you wander off to fight all by yourself. Something tells me you wouldn't stand a chance."

Martin nodded. "We can take my car if you want."

Tanner pushed past Martin and trotted down the wooden stairs. "We started this ride on the Harleys. I guess we'd better finish it that way."

Martin followed the old biker and took the grassy pathway to the garage.

Tanner fired up his Knucklehead and stowed the .44 in the left saddle bag. Then, he eased the bike onto the driveway.

With an uneasy feeling in his gut, Martin followed. Tanner was a loose cannon, and Martin didn't like the idea of the old biker carrying a gun, but he suspected Tanner was right about one thing. Martin would not stand a chance without him.

CHAPTER EIGHT

May 5, 2020, 3:15 p.m.

John took a deep breath and mentally prepared himself while checking his appearance in the car's mirror. He looked much younger than his sixty-plus years, a feat he had to admit was impressive, given the life he'd led. Not that he drank, smoked, or spent time at late social gatherings. He had done none of that. His afflictions were all job related, and his appearance, deceiving.

He climbed out of the car and started toward the door, trying to rid himself of excessive thought. Mentally reviewing the task would only make it more difficult.

Someone opened the door just enough to allow her to see without being totally exposed.

With practiced efficiency, John studied her face. The lady of the house, he presumed, a woman with reddish hair and inquisitive, green eyes. Her face spoke of a kind nature, and John was immediately taken with her and felt sorry that what seemed a good, above-average citizen should be caught up in all of this.

A short time later, John had both Luke and Susan Taylor sitting around the dining room table, peacefully answering his questions. He was good at what he did.

As with Chris and Jennifer Barnes, however, John quickly concluded that Susan Taylor had no clue about what was happening. Luke, on the other hand, presented more of a challenge. He was essentially a child—around six or seven John estimated—living in a teenager's body. He was at least six feet tall and weighed around two hundred pounds, if John was guessing correctly.

"Martin is a good father, Mr. Rainbow, a wonderful husband, and, if the truth be known, a very capable man. He just doesn't believe that or believe in himself. That's the trouble with Martin."

"Where is your husband, Susan? I'd like very much to talk to him."

Susan Taylor didn't answer, which was highly unusual. John repeated the question multiple times with the same result. When pressed, Susan repeatedly said she couldn't give that information. Either she could override the drug, which was also highly unusual, or she just didn't know. Then again, if it were as simple as not knowing, she would easily have acknowledged that.

John pushed away from the table and entered the living room. The open-concept layout enabled him to monitor Susan by glancing over the large granite bar separating the two spaces. He chose a black leather recliner and lowered himself into it. The events of the day had left him tired. He closed his eyes, for only moment with the awareness that he could not allow himself to fall asleep in such a situation.

"Mr. Rainbow?"

John opened his eyes to find Luke Taylor standing over him, an innocent—or perhaps not so innocent—hulk of a boy leaning close, looking intently into his face. John sat forward and gathered himself.

"What is it?" John asked, unable to come up with a better response. The boy should have been sitting quietly at the table as his mother was. "Did you drink anything from the soft-drink can you had in front of you?"

"I no like it."

John considered that. No one had ever mentioned the drug having a taste, either bad or good. "I see. Well, what can I do for you, Master Luke?"

"You help my dad? Bring him back?"

John nodded. It was at times like this that he wished he were a banker, a real estate salesman, even a merchant marine, anything but the harbinger of bad news. "I will try," he said, "but I can't promise anything. You see, I don't know where he is. Maybe you could help me with that. Do you know where your father is, Luke?"

Luke shook his head. "I think he's dead. Maybe. I don't know."

John wanted to say he couldn't bring anyone back, and neither could anyone else in the normal course of things. But he didn't deal in normal.

"Why would you say such a thing, Luke?"

"We had a wreck."

"What kind of wreck?"

"In a car, Dad's car."

John considered the information briefly. "Were you involved in the accident, as well?"

He nodded.

"You seem okay, "John said. "Were you injured?"

He shrugged. "I guess not. Airbag went off too."

John relaxed into the chair. Going on the assumption that Luke and his father had been involved in an accident, it wasn't out of the question that Luke would be unharmed. He had heard of such things before. It might also explain Susan's odd response. Being under the influence of the drug and answering as honestly as possible, Susan would not know for certain where her husband was, at least not in a spiritual sense.

"When did this accident happen, Luke?"

"Yesterday."

It was easy to like Luke, easy to talk to him, which made following protocols, staying neutral and as uninvolved as possible, that much more difficult for John. He'd never had anyone circumvent his interviewing techniques. A disturbing thought occurred to him.

"Tell me, Luke, have you had any déjà-vu moments lately?"

"What that?"

"You know, like when you think you've done something or seen something before, that kind of thing. Maybe you were doing something, and all of a sudden, it was like, 'Hey, I've already done that.' Have you felt anything like that, my friend?"

"Maybe. Yeah, like that."

"Good, Luke, very good. Could you tell me about one of those times, something that's happened within the last couple days?"

"I no go back."

John waited, but apparently that was all Luke had to say. "I'm sorry, but I don't understand what that means. You went somewhere, and you don't want to go back. Is that it?"

"I no go back."

Luke's means of communication clouded the issue. However, there was little doubt in John's mind about the importance of the conundrum he had just uncovered.

Don't give yourself too much credit, John. Luke actually volunteered the information.

Andrew was adamant about residual memories and what should be done about them. No amount of crossover could be tolerated.

"Okay, Luke, you don't have to go back. I promise."

Careful, John.

Where or what, or more correctly, what time and place the boy did not want to revisit could prove important, even invaluable, in discovering the source of the rift. John could, he suspected, insist on Luke consuming the doctored soft drink. Having him do that, however, would not solve the problem. The drug was effective with ordinary memories. Unfortunately, crossovers were an entirely different issue. He should try again.

"Luke, what exactly do you not want to go back to?"

The boy gave John a curious look, almost as if he were catching on to the importance of it all, though John doubted that was the case.

"You like hummingbirds?"

"Hummingbirds?"

Luke pointed toward the back patio, visible through the windows. "They come back. They eat sugar. Maybe it too early. I like hummingbirds, like little Pegasus."

John sat forward, Luke's words grabbing his attention. Project Pegasus was at the very heart of his world. "Pegasus seems a funny name for hummingbirds. Why do you call them that?"

"My dad like it. He gave me a sign."

"What kind of sign?"

"A red horse with wings." Luke nodded, a broad smile spreading across his face. "I show you."

With that, Luke turned toward the hallway leading from the living area and disappeared through an arched opening.

With both curiosity and worry, John followed the same route.

In his bedroom, Luke proudly pointed to a white porcelain sign hanging on the wall above the bed. The pump plate read, *Mobil Gas*, in blue letters, with an image of a red flying horse above—a representation of Pegasus, the winged stallion of Greek mythology.

John was no expert on antique signs, but it looked to be the real deal, except it was smaller than the signs John had seen on television programs.

"That's beautiful, Luke. Where did your dad get this?"

Luke shrugged. "Antique place, I think. He got it for me. I like the horse. Hummingbirds look like tiny horses, flying horses."

John had never heard anyone compare hummingbirds to tiny flying horses. "I'd like to ask you about that place where you don't want to go, Luke. I know it makes you uncomfortable, so I will ask only once, okay?"

"I guess."

"Regarding this place you don't want to go back to, have you been there more than once?"

He nodded.

"How many times, Luke? How long has this been going on?"

He shrugged. "Two, I think. Not long."

"Good, Luke, you're doing fine. Now this is important, so try to answer correctly, okay?"

"Okay."

John paused, trying to be precise without going over Luke's head. "Have you been to this place more than once because you had one appointment or reason to go, or was it the same thing, like 'Wait a minute. I've done this before'?"

"Yeah, like that."

John nodded, close to certain now that Luke had traveled and remembered at least some of it. Such a revelation would worry Andrew to the breaking point. Whatever actions John took, he would have to proceed with caution.

"Very good, Luke. One more thing, was anyone with you when you discovered you were having this unusual do-over?"

He nodded. "My dad. We had a car wreck."

John took in a deep breath and let it out slowly. Discovering two travelers in one day was a bit much, even for someone with his experience. "So, was it the automobile accident...is that what happened more than once?"

He shook his head. "Only once."

Caution, John. Proceed with caution.

"And what preceded the accident?"

He shook his head.

"What I meant to say was, what happened just before the car wreck? That's it, isn't it, Luke? It's right before the car wreck that has you troubled?"

"I no go back."

"No, you don't have to go back."

A tear slipped from Luke's eye and rolled down his cheek. "You said you ask once, no more."

With that, John's heart broke. "All right, Luke. I think I've got enough. No more questions. I'll be leaving soon. After I'm gone, your mom will sleep for about five minutes. When she wakes up, she won't remember any of this, okay?"

He nodded.

"Could you do me a big favor, Luke?"

"I guess."

"If you promise not to tell your mom I was here, I promise I won't come back. No more questions. And more than that, I promise you won't ever have to go back to that place you don't like, okay?"

"Okay, promise."

John patted Luke on his shoulder and turned to leave.

"Mr. Rainbow. My dad love me."

John tried to walk away, to remain no more involved than he was, which was already too much, but he could not. He was an investigator, trained to listen, to pick up on the nuances of what people were saying and what they were not. Luke was not saying, 'Thanks for stopping by. Have a nice day.' Luke was asking for help.

He turned back. "Yes, Luke, your dad loves you very much."

"You bring him back?"

At that point, something inside of John gave way, releasing all the emotion he'd kept at bay. Why did it always seem that it was the innocents of the world who suffered?

"I'll try to bring your dad home, Luke. I can't promise any more than that."

With that, John turned and walked out.

John closed the door to Martin Taylor's house behind him but heard it opening again. He did not turn back. It would be Luke, his confused face and questioning eyes calling out, begging for help. If John had to guess, he'd say Luke's entire world revolved around Martin and Susan. It was difficult to leave him this way—his dad, gone in a way he didn't understand, and his mother, loving but completely unable to understand what was happening. He'd always laid the heavy burdens of life onto those who loved him, encouraged by loving parents to do so. Now, Luke's comfortable world had been turned upside down.

After reaching his car, John brought the rented automobile to life and pulled onto the street, all too aware of Luke Taylor's stare through the doorway of his home, watching his only hope for answers fade from sight.

Back at his hotel room, John reluctantly punched Andrew's number into his phone. When Andrew picked up, John said, "We have a lot to talk about."

"Things have taken a turn for the worse, haven't they?"

Though he didn't completely understand why, John hoped Andrew was still in the dark about the troubling affair. He had a way of knowing things before he needed to.

"What makes you say that?"

"I've had a bad feeling about it from the start. Humor me and tell me you have everything under control."

"I'll do my best. My interview of Susan Taylor and her son, Luke Taylor, turned out pretty similar to that of Chris and Jennifer Barnes. Nothing to worry about, neither of them know anything."

It was true. Susan was clueless. And Luke was in his own little world, which would effectively put him in the same category. He wouldn't cause problems because he wouldn't know how to.

"How about the other family member," Andrew asked, "Martin Taylor?"

John considered his answer carefully. He'd been at this long enough to have developed a sense about travel and those extremely rare individuals who had somehow learned to indulge in it. He decided to just lay it out there. "I strongly suspect Martin Taylor is a traveler."

The line remained silent for a long time, and John wondered if he'd lost the connection. "Andrew?"

"You never cease to amaze me, John. In the field for one day, and you've located the source of the problem."

"In a manner of speaking. However, while I think Martin Taylor is caught up in it, I don't believe he is the source of the rift."

"Maybe you should let me in on the facts and let me make up my own mind about it. What did Mr. Taylor say?"

It was John's turn to delay his answer. This was where things would get sticky. "I haven't interviewed Martin Taylor, not yet."

"Why not? what's stopping you?"

"No one seems to know where he is," John said, "including me. I suspect he's traveling."

"I see. Would you please explain why you don't think Taylor is our man."

"All right," John said, "but you won't like it. All I ask is that you keep an open mind and consider the facts."

"Such as?"

"Such as the fact that Angela Stewart and Candy Barnes, who were both mentally challenged individuals, died at childbirth because of the meddling of our mysterious traveling doctor."

"John, how many times have we been through this? Don't you think I've lost a lot of sleep over all of that, too? But you've become obsessed over it. I wonder if your judgement's been compromised."

John resisted the temptation to throw his phone against the wall. "Well, Andrew, if you really feel that way, then why don't you send down my replacement? I already told you I was ready to retire. What do you say? Shall I pack my bags and return home?"

"All right, all right, settle down. Lucky me, my only hope of reaching a resolution with this matter has gone off the deep end."

"That might be funny if it wasn't so close to the truth. Anyway, there's more. Luke Taylor is also mentally challenged. There's a disturbing pattern emerging. Anybody with eyes can see that. Sometimes, I think you're the one who's obsessed, Andrew, obsessed by your delusion that you're always right."

"I'm just trying to do my job, so let's put our differences aside and move forward with what we have. I'll get the viewers involved and see if we can't get a lock on Martin Taylor. I have a feeling he's the key to all of this."

"In that he might provide some answers, I agree, though I suspect finding him might prove difficult, more so than what we've previously encountered."

"Why do you say that? I know you're tired, John, and didn't want to get involved in the first place, so I can understand your reluctance to do what it takes to find Taylor, but I ask you to pull yourself together and give me one more good effort."

"All right," John said. Andrew was wrong about his not wanting to find Martin Taylor. He very much wanted to find Luke's father. Hopefully, in the end, it would be for the same reasons. "Like I said, my experience is telling me there's something radically different about Mr. Taylor, the way he travels I mean. Finding him won't be easy."

"I assume you have some ideas," Andrew said. "I can almost hear the gears turning in your head. So, let's have it. What do you suggest?"

John relaxed his grip on the phone, feeling a small sense of accomplishment.

"I think we both agree the next step is to locate Martin Taylor. The question is, once we do, if indeed we get that far, how do we proceed from there? We could go anywhere from simple observation, hoping to gain useful information; to casual contact, hoping to plant a positive suggestion; to full blown contact, attempting to change Taylor's previous course of action. The implications of any action on our part are practically immeasurable."

"Why do these things always have to be so complicated?" Andrew asked.

"It's the nature of the beast, having to live with the consequences of our meddlesome actions."

"I know, but at this point, involvement seems unavoidable."

"Yes, Andrew, it does."

"I'll make sure the equipment is ready. Let me know when you get back in town."

"You can count on it."

"Thanks," Andrew said. "Just one more thing before you go. I know I don't say it enough, but I appreciate you and what you do. The entire agency does. You're the heart of our operation, John, and that's the truth."

John grimaced. "Thanks. I'll try not to let you down."

And then there was Luke. John did want to let him down either. It wasn't easy being somewhat unique.

CHAPTER NINE

May 5, 2020, 7:00 p.m.

After finishing his affairs in Tulsa, John left his hotel room. A few hours later, he settled into a recliner at his home in Arlington, Virginia, and sipped on a small glass of Scotch.

He was to go directly to the office following the interviews. However, a slight deviation would be tolerated, if indeed discovered. He'd always taken a few hours to prepare—a time to be alone, gather his thoughts, and concentrate on the mission ahead. This time, he would have the luxury of only a few minutes. Out of necessity, he prepared by spending most of his time becoming acutely aware of his rhythms—his internal reference clock.

Internal rhythms varied from person to person. A matter of genetics, John guessed. The Agency's Determination of travel candidates hinged on the rare trait. It helped travelers return to the same reference point they had left. Physicists had made remarkable advances in understanding travel. Nonetheless, the whole sordid affair remained largely misunderstood. Technicians knew enough to pay close attention to the travelers' biorhythms, and before a jump, a team would constantly monitor them to keep the time-reference computers updated.

Along the way, John had learned something quite interesting about himself. He could correct his rhythms and bring them into alignment just by thinking about them—by wishing them to be so. He even played games with the techs now and then just to keep them on their toes. At least that's what he told himself. He was doing them a sort of secret favor. Traveling was serious business. The techs needed to be at the top of their game.

But that wasn't all. By concentrating on a set of predetermined, temporal coordinates, John could adjust his rhythms to appear normal while they were, in fact mimicking the adjusted coordinates. Of course, he always readjusted the rhythms seconds before travel was initiated. He often wondered what might happen if he failed to readjust in time. After all, he wanted as much as anyone to return to the place where he belonged.

Of course, there was much more than time-reference to consider when determining candidates. Nothing more important, but crucial just the same. The big ones were orientation and reorientation. The ability to adapt to another time and place where one didn't belong, and then leave it all behind upon return, was essential for long-term survival. This was where John excelled. It was the reason Andrew referred to him as being *somewhat unique*.

John finished his Scotch and went into his office, where he kept a file containing the details of the fateful, jump he had completed on May 04, 2017—the date of the first rift created by their mystery traveler. He carefully removed the file from the drawer, and laid it on the desktop, where he opened it to the page displaying the coordinates of the 2017 jump and, more importantly, those relating to the 2014 destination. He dared not keep a digital file of such sensitive information. He committed the coordinates to memory before placing the file back into his desk.

Two hours later, a security team escorted John through the doors of a building located on 3701 North Fairfax Drive in Arlington, Virginia. One didn't simply walk unattended into such a place. He was taken to a small room, where he was searched and questioned—more like interrogated. He didn't know any of the officers. They changed so often.

With the briefing completed, two of the security officers accompanied him to the East Wing and took him down a hallway into a sparsely decorated office with no windows.

He turned to the officers and smiled. "That will be all for now, thank you."

John waited while the officers left the room and then leaned through the doorway, watching until the security team turned the corner down the hallway and disappeared. No one else was in the room or the hallway or the whole East Wing as far as John knew. He strolled behind the only furniture in the room, an empty desk with a lamp on it, and opened the door to what appeared to be a coat closet. He stepped inside, closed the door, and placed his hand upon a glass panel. The closet, or elevator, descended.

Ten stories beneath the surface, the elevator doors hummed open, and John stepped out into a vast area nearly devoid of light. Of course, the closing of the elevator doors took care of the *nearly*. John had never cared for the peculiarities of this part of the business.

Moments later, a familiar form emerged from the darkness, and even before he drew near enough to be recognized, his slightly hunched stance and rapid gait gave him away. It was Andrew.

He hurried over and grabbed John's hand. "It's good to see you, John. It's been a while."

It was true. They often talked on the phone but seldom met in person. "Andrew, how are you?"

Andrew didn't answer. He was already leading John toward a ready room before he finished the question. Once inside, Andrew flicked a switch, and soft light filled the room.

John took a seat near the front of a long, shiny conference table. The light was insufficient by design but still a vast improvement over the lighting outside the elevator. From what he could tell, he and Andrew were alone in the ready room.

"So," Andrew said, "where do we go from here?"

John leaned back in his chair. Why did they always have to go through this? Andrew knew perfectly well what was to happen. "As we discussed, I travel back to May, 04 and intercept Martin Taylor, hopefully before he has the automobile accident. I will then attempt to gain information on the time rift through a formal interview."

"And what if he doesn't cooperate?"

"I can be very persuasive."

"I'm not questioning your ability, John. You have, however, continued to insinuate that this might well be a repeat offense perpetrated by the same person. What if Martin Taylor and your mystery traveler are one and the same? If that is true, I don't expect him to be agreeable to an interview."

"They are not the same. Martin Taylor is caught up in this, but he didn't cause it."

"How can you be so sure?"

John leaned forward and placed his hands on the conference table. "It's difficult to explain," he said. "It's just something I know to be true."

Andrew shifted in the chair and frowned. "That's not much to go on."

"We've completed jumps with less assurance," John said, "even gone on missions with no assurance at all."

"You've got me there. Maybe I'm getting cautious in my old age. Just try to come back in one piece, okay?"

John stared at his hands briefly, then straightened his posture. "I don't know that I've ever been in one piece. Maybe that's the secret to my success." He pushed away from the conference table and exited the ready room.

Minutes later, he and Andrew entered the jump chamber. John let his eyes adjust to the darkness before striding toward the equipment. He counted at least five technicians sitting at various workstations around the immediate perimeter. The charge in the room made the hair on his arms stand on end. He'd never cared for that sensation. He took a deep breath and stepped beyond the electromagnetic curtain. At least most described it as a curtain. It had always reminded John of a waterless yet colorful rain shower.

John closed his eyes and offered a silent prayer. No matter how many times he'd done this, it always terrified him. What if he didn't travel to the right place? If he did, what if he failed to complete the assignment? Even worse, what if his efforts made things worse by further deteriorating the timeline?

Just before the jump was initiated, John, playing no games, deliberately changed his mind and concentrated on the predetermined coordinates he'd memorized.

CHAPTER TEN

May 4, 2020, 2:20 p.m.

Martin twisted the accelerator, and the Harley gained speed. He'd become comfortable with the bike, his riding skills easing in like an old friend.

He wondered what might happen if the last few hours could be rearranged. would his cares disappear into the scrub oaks dotting the landscape on either side of the road if things fell...the right way? The thought did not bring him comfort. If rearranging was in order, it would need to happen, as Tanner had indicated, in exactly the right time and place.

And how would he go about doing such a thing? The incident with the shooter in the woods had happened, but Martin wasn't sure if he or someone else had caused it. For all he knew, he had been caught up in a time-slippage phenomenon happening independently, completely beyond his control.

Ahead, Tanner rode, his gray hair twisting like ropes behind him. After overcoming disbelief, he'd slipped easily into accepting the circumstances. Mostly, it was because of his temperament. He was a loner, a biker, and being in trouble was probably second nature to him. He didn't thrive on conflict, but he wouldn't shy away from it either. Martin wished he could be more like Tanner in facing turmoil. Wishing wouldn't make it happen, though. And Tanner wasn't tasked with facing this problem.

It's all on you, Martin. And this time, you can't run away from it.

Watching Tanner, Martin suspected that the man actually thought he might solve things with the .44 stowed in the Harley's leather saddlebag. Tanner hadn't told him much about what else he planned on doing. Martin didn't think Tanner, or anyone else, could shoot his way out of this one. Not unless the .44 doubled as a time machine. And even if it did, Martin inherently knew, even before Tanner had offered his warning, that tampering with time was no small problem, and that doing so would most likely make things worse.

Miles of asphalt and gravel road unfolded in front of Martin's handlebars, and as he neared the neighborhood, he feared that whatever forces he had set in motion by changing the past would continue to get worse and eventually spiral out of control. The only way to stop that was to get back to the starting point, wherever that turned out to be. When they reached his house, he pulled halfway up the drive and shut down the Harley.

The silence engulfing him reinforced just how out of place Tanner and his bikes were in Martin's world. The trouble was, at the moment, he felt every bit as misplaced. As the seconds passed, Martin understood that Tanner had his fears, as well. He'd become uptight when they'd talked about his niece, Candy. And for him, being here meant facing the possibility that Martin was right about her.

"Okay," Tanner said. "This is it. Now what are we going to do?"

"I'd better let Susan know we're here. Then we can have a look around."

Martin leaned the bike against its stand and climbed off. The continued silence of the neighborhood unnerved him. It was early afternoon and slightly overcast. By this time, Luke, if indeed he was inside the house, would typically have come out and admired the bikes. Luke had never ridden a motorcycle. The closest thing he'd ever experienced was his lawnmower. However, anything with wheels always intrigued him.

Martin thought about the doctor's appointment, and pictured Luke, angry and sulking in his room. The abandoned neighborhood increased his anxiety. The lawn was still neatly maintained, and the hedges, trimmed. Then again, he'd been gone for less than a day. What did he expect...a welcome-home committee?

What Martin didn't expect was the apprehensive feeling that overcame him when the front door to his own home swung open. It was Susan who stood in the doorway. However, her hair had gone from reddish brown to blonde. He hadn't noticed that this morning, which could mean just about anything, but he strongly suspected that it had to do with his going back to save Tanner. A couple of steps behind Susan, Luke's smiling face came into view.

"Don't lose your nerve now," Tanner said from behind. "Everything will be fine."

It wasn't Martin's way to display emotion in public, though a desire to do so overcame him as he leaned forward and gave Susan a kiss on the cheek.

"It's good to see you," he said. "You, too, Luke."

Once they were inside, Susan fought off a smile and regained her straight face. "Where have you been, Martin? We've been worried about you. Luke's nearly beside himself." With an expression that did little to mask her concern, she studied Tanner. "And who is this?"

"Name's Tanner, ma'am, Tanner McIntosh."

Luke stepped forward. "Hey, Tanner. I like your place. I like the swings."

Glancing at Tanner with an I-told-you-so smile, Martin stepped out of the foyer and walked deeper into the house. Susan had met Tanner before, though she obviously didn't recognize him now. That wasn't like her. She was good with people and ordinarily had no trouble remembering names and faces.

"Tanner is a friend, Suze. He goes to our church. We painted houses together during the Day of Caring. You've probably forgotten."

She gave Martin one of those looks. That hadn't changed.

"We were worried about you, Martin."

If Susan had been as worried as she sounded, why hadn't she called him? Then, again, he guessed it shouldn't surprise him under the circumstances. Everything was more or less out of sync.

"Luke's been asking about his skates," Susan said.

Trying to read her expression, Martin stepped closer. They had talked about the skates. "It was supposed to be a surprise, remember?"

"Today's his birthday, Martin. How long were you going to prolong it?"

"Until the weekend. We were going to have a double party for you and Luke."

From somewhere in the background, Luke said, "It's okay."

Martin grew angry, something that was becoming more common lately, and he didn't like it. Even Luke had noticed Martin's anger and was willing to forego a birthday present to keep the peace.

"Hey, Luke, do you like motorcycles?"

It was Tanner. The grisly old biker had pitched in to ease the tension.

"I like motorcycles."

"Well then, come on, sport. I left a couple of good ones sitting on your driveway. I'd be glad to show them to you."

"I like motorcycles."

Susan shook her head. "Luke Taylor, you stay right where you are."

Martin stepped closer to Susan. He softly put his hand on her shoulder and gently ran it down her arm, finally grasping her hand. "It will be okay, Suze. Tanner's all right, and Luke will enjoy seeing the bikes. You know how he is with things like that."

Susan didn't answer, but pursed her lips, cocked her head slightly, and nodded. When Luke and his new friend closed the door, leaving Martin and Susan alone in the house, she pulled her hand free from Martin's grasp and took a step back.

"Okay, Martin, you have some explaining to do."

"All right," he said, "but where do I start?"

"You might try explaining why you're hanging around with Sam Elliot's evil twin and not at work where I thought you were."

Martin smiled at Susan's description of Tanner.

"Tanner looks a little rough, but Pastor Meadows always said that Jesus didn't hang around with saints."

She put her hands on her hips, never a good sign. "What about the rest? Why were you not at work?"

"I called you after I'd dropped Luke off here at the house. I told you I was going to pick up a gift for Candy."

"But you didn't do that did you? You went to God knows where and picked up a Hell's Angel. I'm surprised you don't have a couple new tattoos running up your arm. And I still don't know who Candy is."

Martin's head swirled. "That's the problem, Susan. Nobody remembers her, except for me."

Let's not forget about Luke. His memories seem to be a little crossed-over, as well.

That should tell you something, Martin. With all of the stress you've been under, you've probably just imagined this person you call, *Candy*.

"She's real all right. Tanner showed me her grave."

"For God's sake, Martin, isn't that enough? What are you putting that poor man through, and why?"

Martin frowned. "Nothing more than I'm going through. Candy is not supposed to be dead. She's Luke's friend. We were planning on going to her party in a couple weeks. It was to be held at Tanner's place. You've been there, too, Susan. You have met Tanner before."

"No, Martin, I haven't. And Chris and Jennifer don't have children."

"Then how do you explain the grave? Who is buried there if Candy Barnes is not their daughter? Even Tanner, Jennifer's little brother, admits that much—that they had a child, even if it's in a world where she died a few days after being born."

"I haven't seen the grave, Martin. Like everything else you've thrown at me, the only thing I have to take for it is your word."

With that, Martin lost a few degrees of confidence. If he couldn't convince his wife that everything had been turned upside down, how would he ever explain it well enough to gain even a small amount of understanding from others?

"My word used to be enough," he said, "but I guess that's changed."

"No," she said, "it hasn't. "But how am I supposed to believe you when you're speaking incoherent babble? Come on, Martin, telling me this morning that you've already taken Luke to his appointment when you hadn't, talking about children that don't exist, spooky gravesites, and friends I've never met. What am I supposed to think?"

Martin walked to the large windows that overlooked the back patio and yard. Even though he'd known it was too early, he'd let Luke convince him to put out the hummingbird feeders. It would probably be another month before the tiny birds showed up. He put up a feeder last year for the first time because a friend had given it to him and Susan. Had he known the birds would fascinate Luke, he would have done it years ago.

"I'm not crazy, Susan, though I can't say I blame you for thinking that. I suppose, if I were in your shoes, I'd think the same thing. I wish this hadn't happened to me, wasn't happening to me. But it is. God knows why, but it is."

Knowing he should stop there, but being unable to, Martin continued. "Worse than that, I think I'm responsible or at least involved in some way. Luke and I did go to his appointment, Susan. Luke told me some disturbing things that happened with Doctor Stewart. I guess I let him take too much of my attention."

"Martin, please stop. This is nonsense. You've been under a lot of stress. Dear God, you're having some kind of breakdown."

"We had a wreck, Susan, a head-on collision."

"Can't you see how crazy that is? Luke is just fine, and you're here aren't you, talking to me, and what about your car? Your car was fine this morning. I saw it myself, watched you and Luke pull out of the garage. There was no accident, no car wreck."

Turning away from the window, Martin walked back to Susan. He gently took both of her hands in his. "We crashed, Susan, with enough impact to kill us both. I'm here because I wished so hard for it not to happen the way it was going to. I came back, Susan. I let the air out of Doctor Stewart's tires and prevented him from coming after us. I stopped the crash."

Susan's face lost several shades of color. "I think you need to talk to someone, Martin. I think you need to see a doctor."

A feeling of helplessness snaked through Martin. Susan wasn't buying it, not one bit. He let go of her hands. "Maybe you're right," he said. He turned away and started toward the door. "I'd better check on Luke, see how he's doing."

"I love you, Martin. I'm just worried about you, that's all. Will you do what I suggested, get some help? This is serious, sugar. If you want, I'll make a few calls and find out what we should do."

At the door, Martin turned back. "Hold off on that for a while, okay? Just a few days, that's all I ask."

Susan's expression softened, but not much. "I don't think that's wise," She, said. "This is serious. You could hurt yourself, maybe even harm others. I don't know."

"You know me better than that," Martin said.

"All right, Martin. But I don't like it. Seems to me this is pretty serious and nothing to play around with."

You've no idea, Martin thought.

"Thanks," he said. "It'll all work out, Suze. I promise. I'll get Luke."

Before Susan could mount another objection, Martin opened the door, stepped outside, and walked to the driveway, where Luke and Tanner were busy admiring the Harleys.

"Tanner my friend," Luke said.

Martin smiled. "What do you think of the Harleys?"

"I like motorcycles. I like Tanner."

Martin motioned to Tanner then walked a few feet away. Luke glanced their way, but as Martin had hoped, he was too enchanted with the motorcycles to follow them.

"We've got trouble," Martin said. "I tried to tell Susan what was going on. She didn't take it well. She wants me to see a doctor, and she's serious. I think I convinced her to give me some time, but I'm not sure that she won't call someone."

Tanner nodded. "If you hadn't just saved my life, I might have agreed with her. She's a good person, Martin. You've done well. You can't blame her."

"I know, but my visiting a shrink right now is not a good idea."

"We've got other problems," Tanner said. "Luke asked me about the playground equipment, like you did. He also asked about Candy. I don't know how much he's told Susan. Could be why she's so upset. She might even call the cops."

"I don't think she'd do that," Martin said, "but she's serious about the doctor thing. It probably wouldn't hurt to humor her and go along with it, but something tells me my time would be better spent elsewhere. No pun intended. But time matters, no matter what line you're in."

"Candy scared. She told me."

It was Luke. Martin had no idea how long he'd been listening. "What do you mean Candy's scared, Luke? Have you seen her?"

"Not today. But the other day. I talked to her on my phone. She scared. She no want to go back. I scared too. I no go back."

Martin looked straight into Tanner's eyes. "If that doesn't convince you, I don't know what would. What do I do? I can't leave Luke and Susan alone like this, but I think I might have to. Tanner, if I've caused any of this, had a hand in any of it, I have no choice but to try to put things back where they belong, even if the end result is not to my liking."

Tanner rubbed his chin and nodded. "I reckon you could come home with me, stay there tonight. You've already created, then changed one time fragment that I know about. No reason why you can't do it again. I've been thinking, though. You've got a good thing here, with the family and all. And my life's not so bad. I've got Becker and a business I love, working on the Harleys. Why not leave things the way they are and just roll with it?"

"That same thought has crossed my mind several times. How about I keep the Harley overnight, bring it back first thing in the morning?"

"Not a problem, sport. Now you're talking."

"It shouldn't take much to smooth things over with Susan."

Tanner nodded. "See you tomorrow, then."

Martin turned and walked to the house. He decided he would stop talking about it for a while. Maybe everything would turn out okay.

As Martin crossed the threshold, however, an odd sensation of walking through a fine mist, like walking too close to a waterfall, came over him. He turned to ask Luke if he had felt it too, but Luke was not there.

Martin ran back to the driveway, where Luke must have stayed to talk with Tanner, but he wasn't there. Tanner was gone too, along with the motorcycles.

Turning back, Martin again went into the house, though a sick feeling formed in the pit of his stomach as he saw Susan in the foyer running toward him with outstretched hands, her eyes red and moist. As she drew within range, Martin reached for her, but like a ghost, she faded into nothing.

Then the walls around Martin also disintegrated as if the world were only a thought in his mind, a hologram projected onto the mist he'd walked through, now blown away by some cosmic wind. Martin did not lose his awareness. If anything, his senses were more alive than ever, including his sight, though he could see only darkness. An overwhelming fear that he might float forever alone in an empty expanse threatened to rob him of his senses. A single sensation, however, gave him hope, something to cling to. Susan and Luke were nearby, though he could not see them. It was true, though. He could never mistake the sweet scent of Susan's perfume.

CHAPTER ELEVEN

May 4, 2020, 5:00 a.m.

John's impatience grew as the people in front of him stood and clattered about the aisles, lacking even a snail-like movement toward the exit. He didn't know why he was in a hurry to disembark from flight 207 to Tulsa. It was only a two-hour flight. He had plenty of time. But why did so many of the passengers feel as if they had to take off half their clothing to gain a small amount of comfort, only to search every overhead bin to again find the stuff?

When forward movement finally began, passengers hurried down the aisle like water freed from a hose.

Exiting the air bridge, John entered the terminal and went directly to the car rental area. Minutes later, he pulled the Medina, a subcompact with a stick shift, onto the highway. He hadn't known the rental fleet would include stick shifts. Most people didn't drive them anymore, and many wouldn't know how if forced to. He blew it off as bad management and drove by memory to Mulberry Avenue in Broken Arrow.

Later, John pulled to the curb across the street from Martin Taylor's house, hoping the rental car wouldn't draw attention. He'd never seen one like it.

According to John's calculations, Martin and his son should be leaving the house around 8:30 a.m. He had over two hours to wait. He now wondered why he'd allowed himself such leeway. Of course, he wanted to be sure he didn't miss Martin, though he couldn't recall being this cautious before. More than a few things had seemed off-kilter since the jump, small things, such as his irritation on the plane and stick shifts at the rental agency. He was about to conclude that an error had corrupted the jump when the garage door to Martin Taylor's house rose, followed by the Audi backing out of the driveway.

A man occupied the driver's seat with a passenger.

It could be Martin and Luke Taylor. John put the Medina in first gear, let out the clutch, and followed the Audi. With the time showing just shy of 7:00 a.m., John wondered if his being early had been coincidence or involvement of the technicians.

About ten miles later, the Audi exited the highway, rode the feeder road for a short distance, and swung into a complex of buildings. As the Audi pulled into a parking spot, John grabbed a space nearby. It would have been a safe distance had they not been the only two cars in the lot. It was a medical complex, so nothing would happen for at least three hours.

The door to the Audi swung open and an attractive lady with blonde hair stepped out. Even though her hair color and style differed from before, John had no problem recognizing Susan Taylor. That wasn't all. Judging by the look on her face, she recognized John, as well. At the very least, she had realized he was there and didn't like the looks of the situation. John thought she might get back in the car and drive off. Instead, she slammed the door and started across the lot toward him.

She strode to the driver's side of John's car and motioned for him to roll the window down.

"Do I know you?" She demanded.

"I don't think so," John said. And it was true. Even though he knew her, she should not, based on John's experience, know him.

"Why are you following me?"

"I'm sure it only appears that way," John said. "In all likelihood, we both have an appointment with one of the doctors here."

"It's awfully early for a doctor's appointment," Susan said. "I think you're following me, and I intend to do something about it."

"Wait a minute," John said. He rubbed his forehead, a bout of dizziness running through him. When he looked up, he did not see one Susan or one parking lot, but multiple clones. As a child, he'd seen an old horror movie in which the perspective of the camera was that of a housefly. Through numerous tiny eyes, the audience was shown an array of dizzying images, a kaleidoscope of snapshots, each one differing slightly from the others.

John tried to get out of the car, but the dizziness was too great. His nightmare had been fully realized. The jump had gone wrong. He had to contact Andrew. He had to get back to Arlington and return to the reference point. Maybe in the movies one could seek a magical portal that showed up when needed, but reality was not so convenient. He reached for his it was gone.

"Do you have a phone?" he asked. "I need to make a call. It's extremely urgent."

Some of the Susan's gave him perplexed looks, while others answered in the affirmative. John got out of the car and stumbled toward a Susan, one who held out a phone for him. He heard some others say, "A phone? Well, not on me. There will be one in the doctor's office, but it's awfully early."

John took the phone and fumbled the numbers onto the keypad. Someone came on the line. Perhaps it was Andrew. "Things have gone wrong," John said. I can't make it back on my own. Are you there, Andrew?"

John received no answer. He returned the phone and stumbled back to the car. He couldn't take the chance that Andrew had received the message. He'd have to make it on his own. Travel took a strong electromagnetic field, and the type of equipment he needed existed in one place. He started the car and drove toward one of the Susans. If he could make it to the airport, he should be able to get a flight back to Arlington.

CHAPTER TWELVE

May 4, 2020, 7:00 a.m.

Martin trembled in fear as he floated within the empty chasm, its dark energy pressing against him. It was up to him to solve this dilemma and put things back in order before it was too late. He was only sure of one thing: the nagging feeling that he had to do something about Doctor Stewart.

The trouble was, he was almost as terrified of facing Doctor Stewart as he was of the prospect of floating for an eternity in this abyss. Once again, Martin conjured the image of the calendar and imagined his grandfather's watch alongside it. Nothing happened, though, and it occurred to him that the other traveling experiences had come during times of tremendous stress; first, to avoid the automobile accident, and then, to stop the death of a friend.

Something slammed Martin's feet, and he struggled to regain his balance against the hard surface thrust beneath him. The darkness remained, but he made out shapes in the immediate vicinity. He could only guess he'd ended up in such a location because he'd failed to conjure up a specific time and place. It wasn't long, however, before he realized he was not in some unknown place but was, in fact, standing in the parking lot not far from the building where he and Luke had gone for the appointment with Doctor Stewart.

Why he had ended up at this location was not a mystery to Martin. He'd been thinking about Doctor Stewart. It was the *how* that puzzled him. He checked his watch, which showed May 04, 7:15 a.m. That explained the darkness. If the day's events followed their previous sequence, he and Luke would arrive here around 9:00 a.m.

"Why are you following me," asked a voice.

The question drifted across Martin's senses, and he turned toward the source.

It turned out that the parking lot was not empty. Two people stood beside their cars, having not a heated conversation, but certainly not a friendly one. Their body language gave that much away.

"Why are you following me?" The voice asked again.

Martin didn't like the sound of it. He started across the parking lot, cautiously approaching the people. He didn't know what he would do if they were having an argument, but he couldn't keep a clear conscience and do nothing.

What he saw next, though, as the details of one of the cars came into view, gave him another reason to pause. A familiar, discolored door and slightly dented rear quarter panel identified the automobile. It was the Audi—his Audi. He didn't know the elderly man, and he couldn't identify the car the man drove. But he could never mistake the silhouette of the person standing near the Audi. He quickened his pace, calling out to her as he drew near. "Susan?" Martin shouted in disbelief. It's me, Mar tin!"

Martin walked closer, but Susan gave no indication that she had heard him.

The tall, elderly man glanced in Martin's direction. He did not look directly at Martin, only in the general area, but his movement, coupled with the puzzled look on his face, indicated he had at least noticed something.

As Martin hurried closer, the ground shook and a sound, like that of an earthquake, rumbled through the area. Right before his eyes, Susan changed, blossoming into many images, each a slightly different version of the woman he loved.

"Susan!" he screamed. The noise level had risen. The shaking ground, he guessed. "What's happening? Can you hear me?"

The many images of Susan remained silent, and they swirled, forming into what looked to be a glittering, windless tornado that rose into the sky, becoming smaller until it disappeared.

The shaking stopped, and the area became eerily quiet. The Audi appeared to be covered in a sort of mist, but it remained where it had been, parked a few spaces from the car that Martin could not identify. The elderly gentleman was still there.

"Who are you?" Martin asked.

The man's expression and the way he kept looking in Martin's direction indicated that he could only sense Martin's presence. A stray thought formed in Martin's mind, and he suspected that the strange man was connected to what was happening.

"I need your help," Martin said. "My world is falling apart, and I can't seem to stop it. Tell me, do you know what's happening to me?"

The man didn't answer. He looked around the parking lot for a few seconds, his face carrying a desperate expression. "There's something you need to do," he said. "I'm going to give you a date. You need to go there and see for yourself. But don't stay more than a few seconds."

"Who are you," Martin asked, "and why is this happening to me?"

"I'm the man at the end of the rainbow. And the date is August 12, 1943.

•   •   •

Martin sat in a hard, uncomfortable seat and gripped the handles of a small two-barreled cannon. Sweat slipped from his armpits as he fought to regain his bearings. He sensed a presence and instinctively focused on it. He'd either gone mad, as Tanner had suggested, or his thoughts were tangled with someone else's. He looked at his hands, which were ruddy and covered with short, black hair. His thoughts might be that of Martin Taylor, but his physical being was another matter. He focused on the presence he'd felt earlier. He had occupied the mind and body of someone named Clayton Devereaux, a gunner stationed on board the U.S.S. Eldridge. The date *1943* blossomed in Martin's mind.

"Hey, Clayton," someone whispered.

Martin turned to see two men standing beside Clayton's duty station. He decided to play along. "What do you want?"

"We heard you were scared, don't want to go along with this. Cameron and I have a plan. Thought you might want to join us."

"What do you have in mind?" Martin asked.

"We're getting off the ship before they throw the switches. Why don't you come with us? It'd be the smart thing to do. But you better hurry. We don't have much time."

Martin searched the mind of Clayton Devereaux. A potentially destructive event was about to unfold, something called the *Philadelphia Experiment*, and it had something to do with Martin's traveling.

Claustrophobia welled up inside Martin. This was not his body. He had to get out. He didn't belong here. Dark walls shrouded the edges of his vision and crept closer until he was surrounded in darkness.

• • •

Martin opened his eyes to the parking lot. He looked down at his hands, relief washing over him as he recognized them as his own. He searched for Susan and the elderly man, but they were nowhere to be seen. An eerie lack of sound engulfed the area until footsteps coming from behind Martin shattered the silence. Martin twirled around to see Doctor Stewart walking toward him.

"You look a little lost," Stewart said. "Might I be of assistance?"

Martin glanced toward the area where the Audi had been parked. The car was still there. Whether the keys were in it, or not, Martin didn't know. "Everything is fine," he said, "but thanks for asking."

"Not a problem," the doctor said. "However, you look familiar. I believe I've seen you before. Do you have an appointment today?" The doctor kept his unnaturally black hair artfully disarrayed.

Martin shook his head. "You must be mistaken."

Doctor Stewart's eyes grew more intense. He had the kind of face that was hard to say no to. Had Martin misjudged the man?

The doctor smiled. "I never forget a face. Being a patient of mine is nothing to be ashamed of. You have an appointment, don't you?"

"In a manner of speaking," Martin said. "But the appointment is not for me. It's for my son, Luke. And I want to cancel it."

"I don't see a problem with that. Except Luke will need to make the cancellation. What is the date of the appointment?"

"Luke's not able to do that," Martin said. "And it was for today at nine."

"As I said, Luke will have to cancel it unless you have legal guardianship or power of attorney."

Or we could just not show up.

"I've never formalized it, but I've always handled his affairs, either I or his mother. Luke isn't mentally capable of handling such things."

The doctor's face softened. "Perhaps we can bend a few rules. However, it's a problem you and your wife will need to address. You could run into problems down the road. By the way, what exactly was I to see your son for?"

"It's nothing, really. I carry Luke on my insurance at work, and we just had a change in carriers. The new carrier wants a psychological examination done."

He nodded. "It's always one kind of problem or another, isn't it? Under those circumstances, are you sure it's wise to cancel?"

Again, Martin glanced at the Audi, wondering why he was putting himself through this. He could simply agree to keep the appointment and then ditch it as planned. Then again, there was the matter of Luke's insurance to consider. Doctor Stewart certainly seemed kind and understanding.

And all that logic might mean something, Martin, if you hadn't fallen down the rabbit hole.

"I see your point," Martin said. "I guess I was just getting a little nervous about the whole thing. I'll go get Luke, and we'll see you around nine."

Doctor Stewart smiled. "You've made an excellent decision. Isn't it good to talk these things over? On that note, there's some paperwork you'll need to fill out. Why don't you come into my office and get that taken care of? It will be easier that way. You will have your hands full later when you have your son with you. What do you say?"

Martin did not want to go in and fill out the paperwork, but he nodded his agreement anyway. That was the story of his life, always doing things he didn't want to do. "You're probably right," he said.

Martin cringed when Doctor Stewart put his arm around him, just a casual gesture like that of an overbearing friend, but with Stewart, it felt like shaking hands with the devil. But Martin hadn't completely lost his mind. Martin's world had definitely jumped the track, but he hadn't completely lost his mind. Maybe he would find some answers. He had to find out what was going on, but he'd have to be careful. If Doctor Stewart was involved, Martin couldn't alert him to his true intentions.

The offices were dark until Doctor Stewart turned on the lights. Of course, they would be. It was only 7:30 a.m.

"If you don't mind, have a seat in the waiting area," Doctor Stewart said. "We'll keep this as informal as possible. It should make it easier for both of us."

The doctor was soft spoken and intelligent, and yet, Martin thought he detected a disturbing edge to his demeanor. Martin settled into the same chair he'd used during Luke's visit. The same rips in the plastic decorated the arm coverings. The same black scuff marks riddled the floor. Not much was different, except no one but the doctor was there.

Coming back into the room and handing Martin a clipboard, the doctor said, "It's not that much really, just better to get it out of the way in a more relaxed atmosphere."

It was the same questionnaire Martin had filled out earlier. Or had it been later?

Doctor Stewart sat in the next chair over in a casual manner. He had, however, slipped a white lab coat over his clothes. "Could I ask you a possibly unrelated question?"

Martin shrugged. "I guess so."

"I'm curious as to who that gentleman was you were talking to in the parking lot this morning?"

Already busy filling out the paperwork, Martin paused. "You saw him?"

"Yes, from a distance. Just curious, an occupational hazard, I'm afraid."

"I don't know who he was," Martin said. "He was acting strange, like he was lost or out of place. I was just trying to help."

"Strange, you say? Could you be a little more specific?"

"It's hard to describe. The conversation, if you could call it that, was completely one-sided. I asked him who he was, but he didn't answer. It was like he wanted to but couldn't quite make the connection. I don't know if you noticed, but when he left, he was driving erratically, like he was intoxicated or something."

Letting out a deep breath, as if frustrated by a patient's response, the doctor leaned back in the chair. "I think I had things a bit confused before, but now I believe I'm beginning to understand. Tell me, Martin, are you aware of what's happening?"

A current of fear slipped up Martin's spine. Of course, he was aware. What kind of question was that? It could mean only one thing. The doctor wasn't being fooled at all. He was on to Martin and knew his being there was more than a coincidence. "What do you mean?"

"You actually don't remember any of this, do you?"

He remembered all right. Trouble was, he didn't want Doctor Stewart to know that. Then again, maybe he should tell him. The doctor, while slightly distant and aloof, didn't seem dangerous or threatening.

"And what if I did remember, Doctor Stewart? What would that mean?"

"It's difficult to pin down at this point. Perhaps this will help. Does the name Angela Stewart mean anything to you?"

Martin searched his memory and then shook his head. "It doesn't ring a bell. Why do you ask?"

"How about Sylvia Stewart, does that jog your memory?"

"No," Martin said, "but each person you asked about has the same last name as you. Are they family members?"

"Perhaps they could be, if it helps you to think about it that way."

"I wasn't thinking about it in the first place. You're the one who brought it up."

"Tell me, Martin, how long have you been experiencing these problems?"

Funny you should ask, Doctor Stewart. As a matter of fact, it all started right here.

"What problems are you referring to?"

"Come on, Martin. I might be able to help you if you will cooperate."

"Help me with what?"

"Don't play games, Mr. Taylor. You know full well I'm referring to your delusion of reliving this day."

Martin fought an urge to blurt it all out, tell the doctor everything. "I don't know what you're talking about," he said, "but something tells me you might be experiencing similar problems. Otherwise, how would you have known to bring it up?"

"I know because I'm a psychologist, Martin. And what you're going through is not as uncommon as you might think."

Martin checked his watch. Only a few minutes had passed since he'd come into Doctor Stewart's office. It seemed much longer. "I appreciate your concern," he said, "but I really should be going. I need to go home and get Luke, make sure he's here and ready for his appointment. By the way, how long do you think it will take for Luke to go through the examination?"

"Less than an hour, I'm sure. However, we can reschedule his appointment for later in the day or even move it forward a few days. We have more pressing matters to attend to at the moment."

Pretending to be calm and unconcerned, Martin glanced at the doors. He didn't think they were locked. Doctor Stewart had entered the office in front of him. He'd simply turned on the lights and walked in.

"What matters would that be?" Martin asked.

"We need to take care of your delusional state of mind, of course. I'd be neglectful of my duties if I were to let you walk out, without my knowing more about your situation.

Doctor Stewart looked to be in pretty good shape, but Martin might beat him to the door, especially if he could catch him off guard. "I don't think I am delusional," he said.

Martin got a sinking feeling in the pit of his stomach. Was he to spend the rest of his life reliving slightly different versions of the moments surrounding Luke's appointment? Remembering the short jump, he'd made at Tanner's place to stop the shooter, gave him hope.

And let's not forget about 1943.

He needed a distraction, anything that might gain Doctor Stewart's attention. Once Martin was outside, he could run like hell and find some cover, somewhere to hide, giving him time to think things through.

And then what, Martin, just keep running, keep hiding? Where will that get you?

Doctor Stewart rose out of the chair and stood, looking down at Martin. "You could be right," he said, "but wouldn't you feel better getting a professional opinion? Be honest with yourself, Martin, and with me. Unusual things have been happening, haven't they? You haven't been yourself lately. Why don't you relax and tell me all about it?"

Martin nodded. His current situation was not going to improve and would likely get worse. He had to do something. "Maybe you're right," he said, "but I need to call Luke's mother and let her know his appointment has been rescheduled."

"Not a problem. I'll have my receptionist take care of that. He will be in soon. He's very efficient, don't you think?"

"I'm sure he is. Say, you wouldn't happen to have some coffee around here, would you? I could sure go for a cup right now."

The doctor smiled. "I think you're just trying to get me out of the room for a moment."

You got that right, Martin thought. "Why would I do that?"

"You tell me. Better yet, let me guess. As soon as I'm out of sight, you're planning on making a dash for the exit. Don't play mind games with a psychologist, Mr. Taylor. You will lose every time."

"Maybe so, but you can't hold me here against my will. It's against the law."

"So, now you've become an expert on the law as well? Don't be so sure about that, Martin. It could be that, in my professional opinion, you've become a threat to yourself and those around you. Perhaps I was only trying to do my job until the authorities got here."

"What authorities? You haven't called anybody. And something tells me you won't because you're more afraid of them than I am."

Doctor Stewart laughed, not just a snicker, but a genuine expression of what he must have thought hilarious.

Martin took the chance. Stewart's frivolity probably wasn't the break he was looking for, but it might well be the only one he'd get. He jumped from the chair, shoved Stewart against the wall, and bolted for the exit.

Moving fast, Martin reached the doors and pushed. Through the glass, he could see the brick steps leading to the parking lot and the green shrubbery in the gardens beside the walkway, but the doors did not open. Somehow, Doctor Stewart had locked them.

Martin's biggest fear was getting into a physical confrontation with someone. When he was in school, some kids had been taunting him. He'd had enough one day, so he fought back, laid into one of them. After that, they'd all ganged up on him and had nearly beaten him to death. He'd spent two days in the hospital and had been terrified of fighting ever since.

Stewart had already regained his footing and was coming forward fast.

They were doors, but they were glass doors. Martin didn't think an entrance to a doctor's office, glass or not, would be constructed to leave it vulnerable to breakage, but he didn't let that stop him. He took a few quick steps back and lunged forward with all his might.

The doors burst open with a bank. Martin rolled to the ground but scrambled to his feet and stumbled clumsily down the brick stairs. When he reached the parking lot, he ran. He hadn't known he could still move that quickly. He ran until he reached the corner of the building. Then he turned and ran along the side. He didn't know where he was going, just that he had to put some distance between himself and Doctor Stewart. At some point, figuring he was only running deeper into the complex, he turned left and then left again when he rounded the next building. A few minutes later, winded and exhausted, he stopped.

He had made it to the parking lot, but he was still quite a distance from Stewart's office. He didn't see the doctor or anyone else. What he did see gave him a small amount of hope. Sitting on the far end of the lot was the Audi. No other cars were around it. It was still too early. He'd be an easy target if he went for it now. However, if he waited until the lot filled up, he could probably get to the car unnoticed. Not far away was a small garden. Martin made his way there, sat upon the grass behind a shrub, and waited out of sight.

There was no getting around it. He was caught in a time loop. The gravity of his situation settled over him like a bad diagnosis. The only way out of this was for him to do as Tanner had suggested: find the starting point and reverse whatever had pulled him into this. He sat on the grass for a long time, covered in more fear than he'd felt since his beating at school. He'd been snatched from his happy life and thrown against his will into a nightmare.

The sound of voices caught Martin's attention, and he rose to his feet.

The sight of a group of people strolling across the lot was enough to make Martin think of his family. It was then that a new fear rose in him. Since he was reliving the past, what was to become of the future? More importantly, what was to become of Susan and Luke? Susan played a good role of being tough and resilient, but Martin knew her better than anyone. She was tough, but when she met her match, she had a way of crumbling...and crumbling hard. Martin had no choice but to make things right for her and for Luke.

CHAPTER THIRTEEN

May 3, 2014, 7:00 p.m.

As soon as Martin took a sip of beer, he knew something was wrong. It had been years since he'd drunk apart from the beer he'd had with Tanner, and now here he was in a restaurant, sitting alone at a table and holding a frosted mug in his hand. He couldn't recall having fallen asleep or even having been asleep, but the dreamlike quality of his surroundings could not be discounted. The last thing he remembered, he had been hiding in a garden near Doctor Stewart's office, hoping Stewart wouldn't find him.

The large windows of the restaurant overlooked a small, manmade lake, and a beautiful reflection of blues, reds and greens drew Martin's attention. It was just a highway sign, but the water blurred the colors, transforming the lake into an impressionistic rendering that created an air of romance. It was the restaurant where he and Susan had dined on her birthday. The trouble was that it had been a few years ago. He couldn't pin it down exactly. He'd never been that good at remembering dates. The irony struck him, and for a moment, it seemed almost funny, but there was nothing humorous about the situation. And where was Susan?

The answer came quickly. Susan rounded the corner, glided across the floor— at least that's the way it looked to Martin—and sat next to him.

Martin reached over and took Susan's hand in his. He realized he was staring at her and glanced away briefly. When he turned back, he said, "You look absolutely stunning."

She smiled with a hint of seduction. "I don't know what's gotten into you, but I hope it stays. I'll have to freshen my makeup more often."

Martin didn't know what to say. He was like that, quiet and low on conversation. It had never seemed to matter much to Susan. It bothered Martin, though. He wished he could be more outgoing—more talkative and interesting. He started to ask if she had ordered yet, but didn't in case she had. He didn't want to seem completely out of touch.

Then, Martin got another surprise. A familiar voice came from behind, and he glanced around to confirm his fears.

Doctor Stewart sat at the table directly behind him.

Martin quickly looked away. He didn't think Stewart had noticed him, but he couldn't be sure. The result of his being seen by Stewart could be disastrous.l Even in Martin's crazy world, Stewart's being there was too much for coincidence. Had he been there all along? Martin wouldn't have noticed him back in that timeline because he hadn't yet met him. Or was this the original timeline? He just didn't know.

"Are you all right?" Susan asked. "You were getting all romantic on me, and now you look like you've just seen a ghost."

"Sorry," Martin said, keeping his voice down.

"I guess I'm a little distracted."

"By my good looks and charm, I hope."

"That's it," Martin said, and it was true in part. He hadn't been lying when he said she looked stunning. "That dress is flattering on you. You should wear it more often."

"Maybe I will."

The waiter sat a spicy dish of enchiladas in front of Martin. At least the food wouldn't be a mystery. He remembered it as being quite tasty.

"A penny for your thoughts."

Martin smiled. Susan often used that term.

"I love you with all my heart," he said.

She stared at him, as if she couldn't decide whether her quiet and moody husband had changed, and then her lips quivered into a smile. "I love you, too, Martin."

From behind, Martin heard someone say, "We have our minds made up. Alice and I have decided to have the baby. We've even chosen a name. We're going to call her Angela."

"I understand your sentiment," Doctor Stewart said. "I'm just trying to point out the gravity of the situation and equip you to make an informed decision."

"I appreciate your concern, but we've made our decision."

"All right, McKinley. But Down's Syndrome is nothing to take lightly. That's all I'm saying."

"Do you actually think we would make such a decision without thinking it through? We realize the challenge ahead of us. We'll make the best of it."

Susan reached across the table and tapped Martin's hand. "You're zoning out on me again," she said. What's going on behind that handsome face."

Martin tried to ignore the strange conversation behind him, but he could no more do that than he could understand what had caused all of this. He'd never been good at lying, especially to Susan. He wanted to tell her the truth. He just didn't know how.

"Sorry," he said. "I guess I'm not myself today."

"That's for sure," Susan said. "Not that I mind the romantic flair. But the way you communicate without speaking could spawn a novel. Don't get me wrong. Everybody uses body language, but you take it to a whole new level."

Again, the conversation coming from Stewart's table caught Martin's attention.

"All right," Doctor Stewart said. "You and Alice are good people. You'll make good parents. And I didn't mean to sound cold or insensitive. It's just that you speak from concept, and I from experience. Real life has a no-punches-pulled way of teaching you how it is. And the way you want it to be doesn't always line up with that. I've seen too much pain and suffering, McKinley, too many broken hearts and busted dreams. Some might call me cynical. I like to think of myself as honest."

Martin brought his attention back to Susan.

"Happy birthday," he said.

"You're a kind man, Martin. A bit mysterious, but in a good way, I guess. I'm glad I'm married to you."

Again, from behind, the sound of a cell phone distracted Martin. The man who Stewart called, *McKinley*, answered the call.

"It's Alice," McKinley said. "She's gone into labor. I knew this was a bad idea. I should have stayed home with her."

"She's not due for two weeks, McKinley. It might just be false labor."

"I'm sorry," McKinley said. "But I have to go. It was good talking to you. We'll have to do it again some time."

After a shuffling of chairs, Doctor Stewart and the other man walked past Martin's table.

Martin looked away, hoping Stewart wouldn't recognize him. Thankfully, they walked by without saying anything.

Martin waited until Doctor Stewart and his friend were out of sight. Now he had a new problem. How was he going to handle this going forward?

"I'm feeling better now," Martin said. "I'll try not to be so spaced out."

"You're an interesting man, Martin Taylor." She checked her watch. "And as much as I'd like to stay and explore it further, we had better go. Luke will be done skating soon. He hates it when we're late."

They left the restaurant and walled hand in hand to the parking lot, but Martin wasn't sure which car he and Susan had driven or even if they owned the same ones. Thankfully, Susan led him to the vehicle, his old PT Cruiser. He fished a set of keys from his pocket. What would he do if he had the wrong ones? Breathing a sigh of relief, he recognized them as the Cruiser keys.

Once inside the vehicle, Martin pulled his cell phone from his pocket. He hadn't thought of it earlier. It was an older version, an iPhone Series 5, displaying the year 2014. He glanced in the car's mirror. He had less gray hair and fewer wrinkles.

After a moment, Susan said, "You'd better get your head together. Luke has an uncanny way of noticing details. He'll pepper you with questions."

Martin backed out of the parking space. Then he drove across the lot and onto the street.

Later, when Luke came running out of the skating rink, he looked different—small and thin. When they arrived home, he sat forward and yawned, but he would not want to sleep.

Once inside the house, Luke ran into his bedroom. He returned to the living room, carrying a book. "Look! Mom got me," he said. The book cover featured Pegasus, the mythical horse, flying over a castle.

Judging from the sheepish grin on Susan's face, Martin suspected she'd played a role in this little caper.

"You read me?" Luke asked.

Martin tried not to smile, but he was helpless to stop the expression from spreading across his face. "All right," he said. "But first you have to brush your teeth and get your pajamas on."

"Okay."

After a few minutes of reading, Luke fell asleep. Martin waited until he was sure before he tiptoed from the bedroom, easing the door shut.

When Martin crawled into bed, Susan was waiting for him. There was no small talk, only kisses.

Afterward, Martin rolled over beside Susan and relaxed into the pillow. Their making love was not unusual, but the intensity of it had been. He couldn't recall when he'd ever been happier, and he wished he could capture that feeling now, that he could stay there with Susan in that time and place. He wouldn't mind living those years over again. Then he'd have six years to prepare for what was to come, and maybe things could turn out differently.

"I didn't think you could be a better father," Susan said, "but I've never seen Luke so happy. And what we just did, it's never been quite like that."

She paused. "Is there someone else, Martin?"

Martin wondered if he'd said something he shouldn't have regarding the future or anything else. "What do you mean?"

"You're not that naïve, and I'm not buying it. But if you want me to spell it out for you, I will. Is there another woman in your life? Have you found yourself a girlfriend?"

Martin shook his head. After several years of blissful marriage, he could not understand where this was coming from. "That was one of the most incredible experiences I've ever had," he said. "No one could ever do what you do, Susan, not for me."

She smiled. "I'm glad to hear that. I feel the same way. But something is definitely going on. There's no doubt that you're Martin Taylor, but you're a new and improved version. Not that the old version was bad, but I'm just saying..."

She rolled over and threw one of her legs across his. "Come on, Martin. You can talk to me. What is it? What on earth has gotten into you?"

Martin wanted to tell Susan. He needed someone to understand what he was going through, and no one else understood him the way she did. What stopped him, however, other than the fact that she wouldn't believe him anyway, was the frightening suggestion Tanner had put into his head. His interacting with anyone or anything could change the timeline. He wasn't exactly sure of the implications of that, but he suspected it wouldn't be without consequences. Then again, he had already interacted with Susan in a big way. There was also Luke to consider. Martin had also interacted with him.

"All right," he said, "I'll try to explain, but you're not going to believe it."

Susan moved closer. "And why wouldn't I?"

Martin scooted toward the headboard and propped himself up. "Because, if our roles were reversed, I'm not sure I would."

"Don't back out on me now and leave me hanging."

"I guess," he said, "the best way to proceed might be to ease into it."

"Ease into what?"

"Well, for starters, the car I'm driving will break down in a few months."

She giggled. "What does that have to do with anything? We've both been expecting that to happen."

"All in due time," he said. "Whatever happens, promise me you'll remember what I'm telling you. You might not believe me now, but when these things happen, you will."

"Martin Taylor, what in blazes are you getting at?"

"That I don't understand it. I mean, who could? But I'll try. It's like this. We'll still be in the house. We will decide not to sell and just stick with it. Later, Dan from church will sell me the Audi at a super good price because the PT quit on me."

"If you're making this up to scare me, I'll never forgive you."

A sickening thought struck Martin. His parents. The accident. "In 2017," he continued, "Mom and Dad will be involved in a car accident. An eighteen-wheeler veers into their lane. The authorities will say, the truck driver had a heart attack."

"Martin?"

"They don't survive, Susan. They'll be gone."

"That's crazy, Martin. I talked with Molly a few days ago. They're fine. Why would you say such a thing?"

"It hasn't happened yet. It's 2014."

A thought struck Martin. "I need to go see them. Maybe tomorrow."

"All right. But tomorrow is Luke's birthday. Just keep that in mind."

"It's never left my thoughts, Susan. Trust me, May the fourth is firmly embedded in my mind. It will happen on Luke's birthday."

"What will happen, Martin?"

"The accident. In 2020, on Luke's birthday, he and I will be involved in an accident, as well. It's what started this whole thing."

Susan sat up and flipped on the lamp beside the bed. In the dim light, her reflection looked solemn. "So, what are you trying to say, that you've suddenly become psychic?"

"Not exactly," Martin said. "Do you remember that old movie we watched a couple of times? It was one of your favorites. I think it was called *The Butterfly Effect*."

"Yeah, I remember. It was a movie about time travel. So, you think you've been traveling through time?"

"That's pretty much the gist of it."

The corners of Susan's mouth fell, and stared at Martin. Then she leaned over and kissed him. After that, she turned off the light and rolled over to go to sleep. "I love you," she said. "Try not to think about it. We'll work this out. We always do."

Martin said nothing more. It wouldn't do any good. His thoughts drifted back to the restaurant and the unusual conversation he'd overheard between Doctor Stewart and McKinley. There had been something sinister about it.

During the disturbing office visit, Doctor Stewart had asked Martin if the name Angela Stewart meant anything to him. He'd seemed extremely interested in Martin's answer. McKinley and Doctor Stewart must be related. Angela had been diagnosed with Down's Syndrome. Martin's stomach churned. Candy Barnes and Luke were in danger.

A trickle of perspiration ran down Martin's side. Had a lifetime of dealing with these specific conditions hardened Stewart or frightened him to the point that he was willing to bypass nature and take matters into his own hands? Stewart could just as easily go after relatives of his victims, such as Susan, and Chris and Jennifer Barnes.

When Martin finally drifted off to sleep, one thought followed him. Doctor Stewart must be stopped.

CHAPTER FOURTEEN

May 4, 2014, 6:00 a.m.

In the early hours of the morning, Martin opened his eyes to the same comforting world he'd gone to sleep in the night before. He didn't have to check his watch to verify that. It was just something he instinctively knew. It seemed the more he traveled, the more adept he became at accepting the ridiculous notion of what was happening.

The sight of Susan sleeping next to him urged him to stay, but the nagging idea of finding the hospital where Alice Stewart was wouldn't let him.

After taking a shower and getting dressed, Martin left the bedroom and tiptoed across the living room to the kitchen. It took him a few seconds to remember how to use the old coffee maker, but he was getting better at adapting.

With coffee in hand, he slipped into the office, flipped on the light, eased the double doors shut. Then sat down in the office chair and turned on the computer.

It didn't take long. There were only a few major hospitals in the Tulsa area. Angela Stewart was at Saint John's. Thankfully, she had yet to have the baby. Martin shut down the computer. If he left now, he could be there in twenty minutes.

"Good morning, Tiger. You're up early."

Martin twirled around in the chair. Susan stood in the doorway, wearing a white terrycloth robe. How long had she been there? "Hey, Suze. I had some work to do. I hope I didn't wake you."

"Are you coming back to bed?"

Susan was quite accomplished at arranging questions that led Martin into a trap. It was best to be as honest as he could.

"I had some business to take care of," he said. "I figured I could take care of it and be back before you and Luke were up."

"What kind of business?"

What are you going to do now, Martin? You can't tell her your time-traveling friends are up to no good at the hospital. She already thinks you're bonkers.

Martin leaned back in the chair. He'd left some things uncompleted at the office. It was six years from now, so it wasn't a complete untruth. "Gary wants them first thing Monday morning. There's no way I can do that unless I run over and finish them this morning. Like I said, it won't take long."

"All right, but it's Luke's birthday."

"I haven't forgotten."

"It's also Sunday."

Martin nodded. At first, Luke had been less than enthusiastic about going to church. Martin and Susan had spent a lot of time and energy convincing him that he should go. Now, he liked going. He was beginning to understand what being a Christian meant. Going to church had become part of his routine. Luke was all about routines.

"I'll be back in time for the eleven o'clock service. And Luke will never know I was gone."

"You gone? Where you go?"

"Luke," Martin said, "good morning, buddy."

"Daddy has some business to attend to," Susan said. "He'll be back. Why don't you go ahead and get dressed so you'll be ready?"

Luke smiled. "I go?"

"It's just some boring old accounting reports," Martin said, "nothing you would enjoy."

"I don't see why he can't," Susan said. "It's the weekend. No one will be there, no one that would care, anyway."

Luke looked Martin in the eye, something he rarely did. "I change my mind."

"Well, you can if you want to, right Martin?"

"I stay here."

"Thank you," Martin said, immediately wishing he hadn't. That made it sound like he was thankful for Luke's change of heart.

"Then you need to get going," Susan said, "so you'll get back in time for church."

Rising to his feet, Martin walked out of the office and headed toward the door in the laundry room that led to the garage, with Susan and Luke following to see him off. He hugged Susan and slipped her a kiss that nearly turned sensuous. "It's only you," Martin whispered. "I promise."

"Be careful," Luke said.

Martin pulled his son into a hug. "You can count on that, my man."

As Martin started the PT Cruiser and backed out of the garage, he reflected on Luke's unusual behavior. He rarely reversed his desires for someone else's sake, and the look of understanding in his eyes had said he knew what was going on. Martin had suspected that he might. They'd been involved in the accident together, and Luke knew it had something to do with time.

Martin took the expressway. When he reached the hospital, he drove into the parking garage and pulled into an empty space on the third floor. He'd gotten lucky. The empty spaces were usually on the upper floors. He found the information booth and waited while a small group of people ahead of him asked where Radiation was.

After minutes that seemed like hours, Martin stepped forward.

"May I help you with something?" the lady behind the counter asked.

"The name is Martin Taylor," he said, "a friend of the Stewart family. I was hoping you could direct me to the room of Alice Stewart."

"Ms. Stewart must be popular. Another gentleman was just here, asking about her, as well."

Martin paused, wondering who else might have come to the information booth, with questions similar to his. Doctor Stewart would already know where Alice was. He was a doctor and gaining access wouldn't be difficult. Then again, if he were up to something, he wouldn't disclose that.

"Just out of curiosity," Martin asked, "was he a tall man with black hair?"

"No. He was tall, but his hair was gray and neatly arranged."

Martin immediately knew who it was. How he would know such a thing was a mystery, but most things were a mystery lately. It was the strange man he'd seen in the parking lot with Susan. The man at the end of the rainbow. He might cause trouble. Martin needed to find McKinley...or Alice...first, and alert them to Stewart's intentions. And something told Martin that Mr. Rainbow might try to interfere with Martin's efforts to stop Stewart.

"Could you tell me if Alice's husband, McKinley is here? We're old friends, but I haven't seen him in years. I was hoping to talk with him, give him my support."

"I wouldn't have that information, but if you go to the waiting area, maybe you'll find him."

"Thanks," Martin said.

Martin followed the receptionist's directions and made his way to the waiting area.

The place was full of people, but the man Martin had seen at the restaurant, the one who Doctor Stewart had called, *McKinley*, wasn't there.

Martin stepped into the hallway and went to the nurse's station. No one was there. An idea struck Martin, causing him to consider something radical. He stepped around the counter, found the workstation computer and used it to search for the name of Alice Stewart.

The information popped onto the screen. Martin jotted it down on a notepad and ran to the waiting area. He would let things cool down before attempting to locate the room.

When Martin thought it was time, he went back to the hallway, but a sensation, a tingling that started at the base of his back and inched up his spine, stopped him. He immediately saw the source of his discomfort: a tall man with neatly arranged gray hair, walking along the same hospital corridor.

"Excuse me," the man said, "might I have a word with you?"

Martin shrugged. "Why would you want to do that?"

"I couldn't help but notice," the man said, "that you sensed my presence as I did yours. Only a traveler could do that." He frowned. "How long have you been traveling?"

Martin started to evade the question but decided against it. "Not long," he said. "In fact, you could say it started today, but not in this time. Can you help me? Do you know how to stop it?"

The man extended his hand. "The name is John," he said, "John Rainbow. You pose a curious question. I have been chasing a traveler for many years, but you are the first one I've actually met. I understand your desire to stop jumping through time; however, only you can do that. By the way, I didn't get your name."

Martin hesitated. "It's Martin Taylor."

John arched his eyebrows. "Ah, I finally meet the evasive Martin Taylor. Are you here because of Alice Stewart?"

Martin stepped back. He had not expected the question. Rainbow could be one of Doctor Stewart's cohorts.

"Are you a friend of the family?" Martin asked.

"Not exactly. I'm here to correct an unfortunate mistake. I work for the government as a one-man temporal, cleanup crew. Question is, Martin, are *you* a friend of the family?"

Sweat formed in Martin's armpits and rolled down his side. He hadn't expected to get caught right out of the starting gate. "All right," he said, "I'll level with you. I think someone is trying to harm Alice, or more correctly, her unborn child. I'd hoped I might prevent that."

John wrinkled his brow. "Are you in any way associated with DARPA?"

Martin shook his head. "I don't even know what that means. Now it's my turn for a serious question. Why did you send me to 1943 aboard some ship?"

"Sorry about that. I didn't know what else to do. DARPA is an acronym for the Defense Advanced Research Projects Agency, the agency that exploits my particular talents. It wouldn't be out of the question for them to employ someone without bothering to tell me about it."

"Never heard of it," Martin said. "My profession is nowhere near as interesting as yours. I'm an accountant in the petroleum industry, or at least I was until all of this started."

"You said the traveling started today?"

Martin carefully considered his answer. What must be sensitive information was being given to him, as if he were someone with high clearance. He decided to play it straight. "That's right."

"How did it start? How do you accomplish it?"

"It's hard to explain," Martin said.

"Do you have a machine, a jump room of some sort?"

Martin shook his head. "It's nothing like that, but it starts six years from now, when my son, Luke, and I will be involved in an accident."

"Interesting," John said. "So, it just sort of happens?"

"That's about right."

"Do you have any control over it?"

Martin thought of the incident when he'd mentally conjured the image of a calendar and his grandfather's watch to go back a few hours to save Tanner from being shot.

"Yes, I do, but not always."

"Interesting," John said. He checked his watch, an old one similar to Martin's. "I'd love to stay and learn more about this, but I have business to attend to."

"Alice Stewart?" Martin asked.

"Indeed," he said. "But you should let me handle it. I have experience in these matters. The ship you asked about was the U.S.S. Eldridge, part of an unusual campaign called the *Philadelphia Experiment*. Look it up. It has something to do with all of this, including your traveling. Now, I suggest you leave everything to me and get out of the hospital as soon as possible. You seem to be drawing attention as we speak."

Martin glanced around.

Two women and a man, probably nurses or doctors, pointed in his direction. He needed more information, but now was not the time. He gave John his phone number and strode toward the elevators.

A few minutes later, Martin drove out of the parking garage. He hoped John Rainbow would save Angela Stewart.

A sobering thought ran through Martin. Candy Barnes and Luke were still in danger. He hoped Rainbow would handle that, as well. If not, it would be up to Martin. He guided his car onto the highway and drove home.

Then, though things were already bad enough, when Martin pulled into his driveway, the shimmering curtain he'd experienced before appeared, and everything became unstable.

CHAPTER FIFTEEN

May 4, 2014, 8:00 a.m.

As Martin watched from his car, the neighborhood where he lived was turning into a colorful, wavering mist. As this was happening, Martin's phone rang, and the voice of John Rainbow came through the speaker.

"Martin, where are you?"

"Sitting in my car in from of my house, but everything is evaporating, destabilizing. It's happened before."

"You're in the midst of a jump, Martin. Try to relax. Concentrate on the destination and your mission. It has worked well for me."

"It's a dark and scary place, much like what I imagine purgatory might be, empty and expansive, completely devoid of warmth, even hope."

"It's the time tunnel," John said. "It takes a little getting used to."

"Forget getting used to it. How do I stop it? Being with Susan and Luke in this time frame is wonderful. I'd like to stay."

"Don't even think about it," John said. "The idea of taking permanent residence in a fragment you created is potentially fatal. Trust me. It never ends well. Your fading-out episodes are evidence of that. However, if you concentrate on the mission, why you traveled there to begin with, you might be able to temporarily stabilize the fragment."

Martin scrambled for answers. His mission to was to stop Doctor Stewart. He closed his eyes and concentrated, though his efforts were tainted with off-topic images.

When Martin opened his eyes, the house had reappeared. He could not stay there. "All right. I've calmed things down. Now what do I do?"

"That's all on you," John said.

Martin squeezed the phone. "My situation has something to do with the Philadelphia Experiment, doesn't it?"

"You're in more trouble than you know, Martin. We all are."

Martin hesitated and then added, "There's something else I need to tell you. You're not the only other traveler I've met."

"You're breaking up," John said. "You've encountered another traveler?"

Martin glanced at his dissolving world. "He's dangerous, John. His name is Doctor Jackson Stewart."

Martin received no answer. "John, are you there?"

There was only silence. The line had gone dead.

With thoughts of Susan tugging at his heart, Martin backed away from his house, then drove through the nearly empty neighborhood. A few neighbors strolled absently along the sidewalks as if they didn't see him. At the intersection, the stop sign rose above the car, pitched left and right and then settled back to a more correct level. Ignoring the ghostly neighbors, Martin continued. When he drove onto the expressway, the road swayed, giving him the sensation of driving on a floating barge.

Later, Martin pulled into the parking lot outside Doctor Stewart's office. The complex of professional buildings loomed hazily before him, shrouded with fog like a painted backdrop in an old vampire movie. A sparse scattering of people, looking much like those in the neighborhood, moved absently along the parking lot and sidewalks.

Martin, got out of his car, and as he walked past a lady holding the hand of a child, Martin spoke to her. She gave no reply or indication that she'd seen him. The child rolled his large, blue eyes toward Martin and shook his head as if to say, *go back the way you came and get away from this place!*

Had the child been an unwilling patient, as Luke had, or was he a time messenger sent to inform Martin of a bad decision? Martin calmed his nerves and walked toward Stewart's office.

Reluctantly, Martin ascended the stairs and yanked the door open before he could change his mind. And just like that, he was back inside the waiting area.

He started toward the receptionist's window, glancing warily at the people inside. They appeared to be much like the other people in the parking lot, distant and unaware of his presence.

Waiting at the windowed counter until it became obvious that the receptionist was not going to acknowledge his presence, Martin said, "Excuse me, sir, but I'd like to have a word with Doctor Stewart."

As if Martin were only a fly on the wall, the receptionist was unreceptive and went about his duties as though nothing had happened.

Martin wondered if he could remain unnoticed. If so, he could walk through the area undetected and go to Doctor Stewart's personal office. He might find some answers there. He casually walked behind the reception area, where he saw a hallway and several offices. He checked each one, knocking softly and looking inside. When he reached the office on the end, the largest of the three, it turned out to be Doctor Stewart's.

Shrugging off his apprehension, Martin ducked into the office and searched the filing cabinets. Seeing nothing of interest, he sat behind the desk and rifled through the drawers, finding a few hastily scribbled notes that might lead to something if he were given time to study them.

Then, a painting on the wall—a reproduction of *The Blue Boy* by Thomas Gainsborough—caught his attention. It was not flush with the wall but hung away from it on the left side.

Martin walked over and pulled the hinged artwork from the wall. Behind it was a safe. He didn't expect it to be unlocked, but when he tried to open it, the thick, metal door swung open. His pulse quickened as he stared into the small, dark opening, unsure of what to do with his discovery.

Shaking off his anxiety, Martin took the contents from the safe, a file and an old-fashioned ledger. He sat in the chair and opened the ledger. On its pages, yellowed with age, he saw several rows of figures, dollar amounts, identified as *The Phoenix Foundation*.

Martin flipped open the accompanying file. In it were several newspaper articles and letters of gratitude related to the foundation. As Martin scanned each document, a lump formed in his throat. The Phoenix Foundation's sole purpose was to gather information and research to aid certain senators—Lincoln Meyer from Connecticut, Ronald Day from California, and Maynard Simms from New York—in designing legislation that would mandate all unborn babies diagnosed with Down's Syndrome or other related illnesses to be aborted.

Overwhelmed by the ramifications of what he'd discovered, he barely noticed the opening of the office door. When his thoughts quit spinning, he looked up and stared into the eyes of Doctor Jackson Stewart.

"Who in blazes are you?" Doctor Stewart asked. "And what are you doing in my office?"

Martin pushed back from the desk and slowly got to his feet. Unlike the others he had encountered, Doctor Stewart could obviously see him. He did not, however, seem to know him.

It occurred to Martin that such a thing was possible because Doctor Stewart had not traveled here from 2020 but from some other date on which they had yet to meet.

"I'm sorry," Martin said. "I went looking for the bathroom and ended up here."

"Is that right?" Stewart said. He walked closer and scooped up the file. "I see you also have some of my personal information. Where did you get that, the toilet stall?"

Martin shook his head. "That's not mine. It must have already been on the desk. I apologize for being such an inconvenience. If you don't mind, I'll go back to the waiting area now."

Doctor Stewart slowly backed from the room but remained in the doorway, blocking the exit. "Sit back down and make yourself comfortable. I've already called the police." He paused, pulling a small handgun from his jacket and aiming it at Martin. "You're not going anywhere until the authorities arrive."

Martin slumped into the chair. Closing his eyes, he thought of Susan and Luke and how much he wished to see them. When he opened his eyes, it was not to a new location. He was still in the office with Doctor Stewart holding a gun on him. Panic set in. In his efforts to remain in this time and place longer than he should have, had he locked himself into the fragment? Minutes later, he heard voices coming down the hallway.

"Thanks for responding so quickly," Doctor Stewart said. "He's right in here. I detained him for you."

As two uniformed police officers entered the room, Doctor Stewart stepped into the hallway.

The officers glanced at each other, puzzlement creasing their faces. "You must be mistaken," the tall officer said. "There's no one here. Are you sure he didn't slip out while you were calling us?"

Doctor Stewart came back to the doorway, where he paused, his head pivoting left and right. "He must be hiding somewhere!" the doctor screeched, his voice rising in pitch with every word. "He was there, I tell you!" He thrust a shaking finger at his desk chair. "Sitting right there!"

The tall officer shrugged. "We've looked everywhere," he said. "We can search the rest of the offices if you want, but I have a feeling whoever it was is long gone by now. I've dealt with this kind before. They're slippery. He'd sneak out unnoticed at the first opportunity."

Remaining quiet, Martin stayed as still as he could. He would leave when he got the chance, sneaking out unnoticed. But when the police officers left the room, everything turned to mist, and Martin was once again cast into purgatory, back in the total darkness of the time tunnel.

CHAPTER SIXTEEN

Monday, May 11, 2020, 10:00 a.m.

The darkness lifted, and Martin was on the sofa in his living room. He hardly ever sat there. His black leather recliner was empty. It had been a gift from Luke when he still worked at Huntington, a workshop designed for people with special needs. He'd used the bulk of his annual bonus. Out of respect, no one else used it, except for an occasional friend or relative who didn't understand it's significance.

Being in the wrong seat wasn't the only reason Martin suspected something was amiss. A menagerie of strange thoughts had begun to flood over him, tender feelings coming from his consciousness. He instinctively backed off, distancing himself from the danger.

Since Martin had started traveling, he'd developed a habit of checking his watch to gain orientation, but when he glanced at his wrist, his watch wasn't there. Instead, he saw a thinner, more feminine arm. Martin considered looking in the mirror that hung on the wall, but before he could, Susan walked into the room. She was dressed in business attire. Martin fought an urge to wrap his arms around her.

"I'm glad you're here," Susan said. "It's an emotional time for Luke. And for me."

An inner will other than his own will caused Martin to rise and approach Susan. He felt his vocal cords move. "You look wonderful, Momma."

Momma? Martin held back, keeping himself in a tight bubble. He quickly formed a mental wall for his protection and that of the host, who he had come to understand was his daughter, Krystal.

Prior to the fourth of May, Martin would have been terrified or convinced he was stuck in a bizarre dream. Now, he knew what to do. He opened a small hole in the bubble and suggested that Krystal check her phone.

She pulled it from her purse. It showed Monday, May 11, 10:00 a.m.

It dawned on Martin what had happened. It was past the fourth of May. He hadn't survived the accident. His pulse quickened. Otherwise, he would have shown up as himself.

"You might want to check on Luke," Krystal said.

Susan nodded and went to Luke's room. "Hey, big guy, are you ready for the meeting with Senator Padgett?"

"I no go."

A sigh of relief ran through Martin. Luke was being Luke, but at least he was okay. But why in the world would he be meeting with a senator?

"Luke, you and I have already been through this. What we're doing will help you and your friends at Huntington. You want that, don't you?"

"I guess. I wear Spider-Man?"

"Tell you what," Susan said, "how about you wear Spider-Man under your dress shirt? Will that work?"

"I guess."

Love and pride surged through Martin. He had always been the one who could handle Luke. Now, Susan had stepped up and filled in. And her way of taking care of the issue was just how Martin would have done it.

Susan came back and hugged Krystal. "Love you, sweetie."

A few minutes later, Luke walked in wearing a nice shirt and tie. His expression indicated his displeasure with all of this, but as soon as he glanced at Krystal, that changed. He walked over and stared at her, as if seeing her for the first time. "Krystal?"

"What is it, Luke? You look a little frazzled."

"Where Dad?"

Susan answered. "He's not here, big guy."

Tears ran down Susan's face. "We'll get through this."

"He okay," Luke said.

Susan wiped her tears away and looked at Krystal, who returned the sympathetic glance.

Martin's heart broke. Luke knew something the others didn't. His matter-of-fact response proved he'd sensed Martin's presence.

"Well," Krystal said, "let's get going."

About twenty-five minutes later, Krystal pulled into the parking lot of some government offices. Martin felt uneasy. What had Susan, Krystal, and Luke gotten themselves into?

They got out of the car and followed a side walk to the front entrance of the building and went inside. After locating the office and talking to a receptionist, they were seated around a long conference table. A few moments later, Senator Padgett, a short lady displaying a determined expression, came into the room.

"Hi, Heather."

It was Luke. He seemed to know the senator.

"Luke. How are you doing?"

"Good."

The senator smiled. "Thank you so much for agreeing to meet with me today. I know it's not a good time for you, but some powerful politicians are hurrying to push this through. It's extremely important we act as soon as possible."

Push what through? martin wondered.

The senator shook her head. "Only a few years ago, I would not have believed anything like this was possible. But after what we've been through with the last two administrations—and I mean the whole Washington establishment—nothing surprises me. There's a good chance they will push this through. If there was ever a time for prayer, it's now."

Martin subtly urged Krystal to inquire further.

"Senator Padgett, what is Luke getting himself into?"

Martin studied Senator Padgett's reaction to the question. She looked as if she'd been caught off guard—surprised the family didn't know what was going on.

"I'm sorry," Krystal said. "I don't know why I asked that. Just nervous, I guess. But how can Luke possibly help with something like this?"

The senator leaned back in her chair. "My daughter, Patricia, worked at Huntington for a few years while Luke was there. Patricia often spoke highly of him. If anyone can pull this off, it's Luke or someone like him."

Of course, Martin thought. He remembered Luke's friend, Patricia. He hadn't known the senator was her mother, though.

Senator Padgett leaned against the table. "Luke is a special young man. He instantly makes friends because he inherently believes everyone is his friend. His simple honesty comes through unlike any other special child I've met. He totally has the power to change some minds."

It was true. Martin loved his son for that quality.

"We're taking the message directly to the people," the senator said. "I've been working with producers to put together some television commercials. We plan to start airing them two weeks from now. If the networks will run them, and that's not a given, we'll reach a lot of people. Once the public meets Luke and understands what's at stake, we've got a good chance at beating this thing. I want Luke to be my spokesperson."

"I do it." Luke said, his voice cracking.

Silence fell over the conference room.

Martin swelled with pride for his son. He had displayed courage.

"Praise God," Susan said. "Luke, you never stop amazing me."

It occurred to Martin that his being in certain places at the right time was more than coincidence.

"Sounds like we have a deal," Senator Padgett said.

Susan stood beside Luke, putting her hand on his shoulder. "You're a brave young man."

• • •

The ride home was quiet but not empty. Martin left just enough of an opening to understand what was going on, but otherwise remained within the bubble. His thoughts—which bounced between disbelief and fear—were scattered.

Krystal gazed around the living room. The recliner came into view. She paused to consider whether she should sit in it and then plopped onto the cushion.

It was then that Krystal seemed to sense Martin's presence. He had tried to be as noninvasive as possible, but he guessed having someone else in your mind, especially someone close to you, would not go completely unnoticed. Krystal glanced at the table beside the recliner where Martin's watch lay ticking. The moment was unnerving but also uplifting. She took the watch and turned it in her hands.

Martin struggled to clear his mind, but he began to lose focus.

CHAPTER SEVENTEEN

Friday, September 15, 1978

When Martin regained his bearings, he was in an old but familiar house. On either side of the overstuffed sofa were two antique tables. To his left, a bundle of logs smoldered in the fireplace. He was in his Grandpa Frank's house. He rose, strode past the stairs to Grandpa Frank's office, and peered through the glass doors. His grandfather sat in a chair behind his desk. Martin admired his grandfather, though he had always felt intimidated in his presence. The man had played football at Central High and, later, at the University of Oklahoma. He had succeeded at everything he had tried. Martin had spent hours during his youth admiring a photograph of the dark-eyed man with the stern, chiseled face. His grandpa now looked to be around thirty-five.

Martin turned toward a large mirror that hung on the wall. As he gazed at the image of a young man, he realized what had happened. He had jumped into his father. Judging from the shocked look on his face, his father also wondered what was happening. Unfortunately, Martin had been much like his father—struggling through life but never able to grasp the brass ring.

Martin quickly put up his mental barrier.

"Billy, come here for a moment."

Martin turned back. It was Grandpa Frank—Frank Martin Taylor III, Martin's namesake—and Grandpa's requests, though never uttered with an edge of anger, were something that everyone always dropped what they were doing to respond to.

"Now?" Martin asked. Or was it Billy who had responded? He wasn't sure.

The sound of shuffling footsteps filtered through the house. Martin turned and saw his Grandma Phyllis approaching. Seeing her unnerved him but filled him with joy. What would he say to her? Would she know he was there and not merely her son Billy?

"What's the matter, hon? You look rather pale."

Martin understood. His Grandma Phyllis would be suspicious. Billy Taylor probably didn't spend much time standing in the foyer, staring through the glass doors of the library.

A smile crossed Martin's face. "Hello, Grand—" Thankfully, he stopped before completing the words. Instead, he closed the distance between them and wrapped his arms around her.

"Oh, there, there," she said. "It'll be all right."

Martin forced back the tears.

Grandma Phyllis cupped Billy's face with her small but strong hands and shook her head. "It's okay, hon. Father just wants to talk to you. He's not upset. He's not the kind to get upset. Now, run along. It's not polite to keep people waiting."

Martin wanted to talk more with his grandma, but doing so would increase the probability of something going wrong. He started toward the library but turned back.

She raised her eyebrows but said nothing.

"I just wanted to tell you how much I like your chicken and dumplings."

Martin studied his grandma's face. Of all the things he could have said, why had that popped out?

She laughed. "Billy, you say the strangest things. You're not acting like yourself, but it'll get better soon. I promise. Now run along."

Grandma was closer to the truth than she realized. Martin's father rarely showed affection or any other emotion.

"Love you, Mom. And you're right. I am a little off-kilter."

Martin hesitated. What choice, other than to respond to Grandpa, did he have? He pushed open the glass doors and closed them.

Grandpa Frank pointed at the couch sitting along the wall in front of his desk. "Have a seat," he said, pulling a cigar from a desk drawer. He trimmed the end and lit it, savoring the smoke, and then said, "If this is about not making the football team, don't worry about it. There will be other things."

Grandpa's words caught Martin off guard. He'd expected that his dad was in for a tongue lashing. But the love and concern on Grandpa's face was overwhelming.

"It's not fair," Martin's dad said. "Kenny Johnston got picked, and I'm tons better than he is. His dad is all chummy with Coach Roberts, that's all."

Martin felt strange, being in the same body with his father. His dad had implied that Grandpa, with his influence, could have gotten him on the team. Martin's dad was just a kid, and kids had a menagerie of confused thoughts, but Grandpa would never wrongfully help someone. Martin instinctively stepped in to smooth things over.

"You're right, Dad. I shouldn't have said that."

Grandpa leaned back in his chair, took a draw on his cigar, and blew the smoke out in one steady breath. He intensely studied Martin's, or rather, his dad's, face.

Fear ran up Martin's back. Grandpa Frank was an intelligent man. 'The things he can do with the stock market,' Grandma Phyllis often said, 'why, it's almost scary.'

"I'm surprised at your shift in behavior," Grandpa said. "There's something different about you." He swept his free arm about the room. "Something strange about all of this."

Grandpa paused and enjoyed another draw on his cigar, wise to the possibility that something unusual might be happening but accepting the situation with ease. It was how he faced everything.

"There's something I've been meaning to tell you, Billy. Your biggest problem, and the reason you don't succeed, is because you don't expect to. You have no confidence."

A plethora of emotions flooded Martin's senses. "I love you,"—he had to fight not to say *Grandpa*—"Dad. I don't think I've ever told you that."

Grandpa Frank smiled. "I love you too, Billy. And I'm sure you've said it before, one way or another. I've never been disappointed in you, son. If I've given you that impression, please forgive me. Life is what you make it. But don't make too much of it."

"Thanks," Martin heard his dad say. "I appreciate that."

"I need to ask you something," Martin said. "I've been thrust into a situation that involves a difficult choice."

Grandpa Frank glanced around the room. "Questions surround us, Billy. An impressive vocabulary for you. What choice are we talking about?"

"A delicate issue," Martin said. "And, as you pointed out, I might not be up to the task. If you had the chance to go back and change something that might help your family, but you weren't sure what the effect on everyone else would be, what would you do?"

Grandpa Frank studied Billy's face. "Whenever I face something out of my wheelhouse, I take it to my Father in Heaven. After that, I keep myself aware and open to subtle suggestions that come in a variety of ways, such as a related newspaper article I chance to read. It's the way He moves in me. Think of this decision like the other problems you must deal with. Face them or run away. Life is full of joy but also riddled with problems. Thinking you can insulate yourself from trouble by choosing to do nothing is unwise. Becoming comfortable with the idea that God, full of love and grace, is on your side opens doors you never knew existed. It brings an understanding of how to operate from a place of confidence."

Martin knew of his propensity to avoid conflict, but he'd never considered the problem from that perspective.

"For you, it would be manageable," Martin said. "But what if I do all of this and still make the wrong decision? What if innocent people suffer because of my error?"

"If you do what you think is right with the confidence of believing in the power of prayer, you have done your best. Living in fear is a prison of your own choosing. Believe me, Billy, if I could solve all your problems for you, I would. But I'm afraid it doesn't work that way. We must choose our own paths, make our own decisions. Otherwise, life is meaningless."

Grandpa spoke as if he was dealing with a business associate, not his son.

"Is it wrong of me," Martin asked, "to take these matters into my own hands?"

"It seems like something you must do. Your mother and I believe in you, Billy. You have the ability to rise above your doubt and believe in yourself."

"I hope you're right," Martin said. "The stakes are high."

Grandpa smiled. "I've enjoyed our talk, Billy. Unfortunately, I need to get back to work. He again surveyed his surroundings, an indication that he suspected something was amiss. I expect we'll talk again soon."

Martin watched his grandfather busy himself with whatever business he had at hand. Then he turned and walked out of the office, closing the glass doors behind him.

The aroma of chicken and dumplings cooking in the kitchen filled the hallway, and Martin subtly reminded his father how lucky he was to have such caring parents.

As Martin's dad walked through the living room, the ringing of an old-fashioned telephone broke the silence, and seconds later, Grandma Phyllis announced that the call was for Billy.

Martin's dad brought the heavy handset to his ear and said, "This is Billy."

The voice of another boy, perhaps a friend of Billy's, came through the receiver. "What are you doing, Taylor? Sorry you didn't make the cut. But, hey, if I had anything to say about it, you'd be on the team."

"Thanks, man."

"Hey, no problem. Me and a few other guys were thinking. You know. We talked about it earlier. We're going to cruise around. Kind of hoped you would go along too. It will be cool. What do you say?"

Martin had stayed in the background during the conversation. He now tapped into his father's thoughts and determined that, sure enough, the boys were up to no good. He didn't think his father would go along with stealing cars. But just in case, he offered a few vivid scenarios of what could go wrong.

"I better not," his father said. "Mom has got a lot for me to do around here today."

Way to go, Dad.

"Hey, I got to go," Martin's father said. "Talk to you later."

A good feeling, one that said he'd done the right thing, swept through Martin's dad.

Tapping into his father's consciousness triggered Martin's awareness, and his mind snapped back to Luke, Krystal, and Susan. Grandpa had been talking to Billy, but Martin had taken it to heart, as well. If ever there had been a time for him to step up to the plate, it was now.

What would Grandpa Frank do?

Grandpa would not avoid the problem. Martin would do the same. He was a Taylor, wasn't he? He would find Doctor Stewart and try to reason with him. If that didn't work, he would think of something else.

CHAPTER EIGHTEEN

Sunday, May 04, 2014
Friday, September 13, 1991

Having decided to follow Grandpa Frank's advice and meet life's problems head on, Martin was left with another problem. If he wanted to talk sense into Doctor Stewart, what would be the most beneficial time and place for that to happen? The more he thought about it, the idea of meeting Stewart early on before he'd become hardened, made sense. That narrowed it down somewhat. However, that still left a lot of ground to cover.

Martin mentally directed himself back to his home office, focusing on the time right after he'd met John Rainbow at the hospital. Martin had operated there without much notice.

Just to be sure he'd landed in the right timeline, he checked the house, going quickly through each room. The house was intact.

Martin went back to the office. As he switched on the computer, he looked through the window overlooking the front yard. One ghostly neighbor glided past, moving aimlessly along the sidewalk.

In that moment, Martin completely accepted his fate. He could no longer pretend it was all a dream or even an elaborate hallucination. He had become a traveler, and with that came an undeniable sense of responsibility.

He returned his attention to the computer monitor, and after a few minutes of research, he had the information he needed. It seemed Doctor Jackson Stewart had attended the College of William and Mary in Williamsburg, Virginia, and on Friday the thirteenth of September 1991, a controversial political rally had been held at the school. It had made the news. Something like that would have drawn Doctor Stewart's attention because he had strong political leanings.

Martin now knew what he needed to do. His experience and his conversations with John had taught Martin that he accomplished his traveling in a different manner than the other two men. John Rainbow and Doctor Stewart remained unchanged by time when traveling. Martin, in contrast, became a younger, or older version of himself and often inhabited the bodies and minds of relatives. The answer wasn't as simple as choosing another time. It would depend on what he hoped to accomplish.

As he had before, Martin formed an image of a calendar in his mind—a large one, the kind one might write significant dates on—and once there, he flipped the pages until he came to September 1991. He would need a few days in which to reach Williamsburg from Tulsa. He chose the eleventh day, and as he mentally put his finger on the target, his surroundings scattered into a swirl of color.

● ● ●

Martin's world resolidified into the warm and familiar setting of his childhood bedroom. Instinctively, he checked his watch. At eight years old, he had worn a wristwatch, not that he would have needed it to check the time. Several clocks hung on his bedroom walls, each one, reading 6:00 p.m. He had the rest of the evening and one good day to get to Williamsburg. Not much time. The clocks were not a surprise, but their significance had not struck him until now. He had always been fascinated with time, and now he was literally part of it. He formed a mental barrier, though young Martin, as perceptive as ever, had already sensed something wasn't quite right.

The boy jumped off the bed and dashed into the living room, where his parents would be watching television.

Martin suggested subtle but reassuring thoughts of everything being okay.

The boy wasn't hungry, so he must have just finished dinner.

But Martin wasn't there to reminisce about his childhood. He had to find Doctor Stewart. The trouble was, how was young Martin going to get from his home in Tulsa to a college in Virginia? Martin studied his small hands and spindly legs. He'd almost forgotten what it was like to be so small. What he'd thought would be difficult before, now seemed nearly impossible.

He had no wallet, so he checked his pockets and found a grand total of seventy-five cents. Even with 1991 prices, he wouldn't get very far on that.

"Are you all right"? his mother asked from the hall. "Why are you just now coming out of your room?"

A swarm of emotions invaded Martin's senses. He didn't know if he wanted to panic or break into a happy dance. One thing was for sure. He had to answer. "Okay, Mom."

Now what, Martin?

He had to be careful. Something could go wrong. Tears leaked from his eyes. Against his better judgement, he rushed toward his mother and wrapped his arms around her.

"It's so good to see you," he said. "I love you so much."

She immediately dropped to one knee, her hands cupping his face while her thumbs dried the tears. "I love you too, Martin. But why are you crying?"

He fought for composure as his mind raced for answers. "Sorry. I fell asleep on the bed and had a bad dream."

"What kind of dream, dear? I've never seen you like this. You've got me worried."

"It's nothing, really. I'll be okay. Just a silly old dream, that's all. You know, like the ones I used to have." It was true. He'd been prone to nightmares when he was younger.

She smiled, which nearly brought tears again, but Martin fought them off.

"Dad was just saying how good a dish of ice cream might taste. I'll bet that would drive away the bad dreams. What do you say?"

"Sounds good, Mom. Sounds really good."

For a moment, she studied Martin's face, as if she wasn't quite convinced. Had she detected something wasn't right?

Martin hesitated. He couldn't just stand there and do nothing. "Ice cream sounds pretty good," he repeated. He'd come to this time and place for a reason, and he had little time to get that accomplished.

He went to where his mom and dad were sitting behind folding TV trays containing bowls of ice cream. A warm feeling settled over him as he comfortably took his spot. His mother had been a stickler about eating at the kitchen table, but ice cream in the evening had been her one exception.

Switching on the TV, Martin's mother sat the remote beside her. Martin's dad had already started on his ice cream.

Martin uttered a silent prayer, not only for the ice cream but also for the opportunity to take part in the weekly event that had been such a special part of his childhood. He wished he could stay and enjoy it, but John Rainbow's haunting words reminded him that he should concentrate on his mission. Timeline fragments, especially those created by travelers, were not stable.

"The ice cream is great, Mom."

Martin's mom and dad shot questioning glances at him. He hadn't been so appreciative as a child. He didn't remember his parents being that perceptive. To lessen his chances of being discovered, he would have to make his move tonight. As soon as everyone was asleep, he would quietly leave the house and make his way to the airport. He sucked in a breath as another thought struck him. Young Martin couldn't legally buy a ticket. In order to get to Virginia, he would have to be a stowaway.

"That was delicious. Could I go to my room now?" Martin blurted out. "I'm kind of tired."

"Well, if you want, dear," said his mother. "But *Home Improvement* will be coming on. You always seem to enjoy that."

Martin lifted the corners of his mouth in a forced smile. He needed time to think, and plan. "That's okay. Dad would rather watch something else, anyway."

"Okay, dear. Put away your bowl and tray first."

Martin did as he was asked and went to his room, hoping his parents would turn in early, too. He sat on the bed and gathered his thoughts. Nothing about this was going to be easy. He'd be lucky if he pulled it off.

Getting out of the house unnoticed would be difficult enough, but the challenge of getting to the airport on foot in the middle of the night was a bigger problem. At least the weather was nice. He glanced at his watch. It was 7:20 p.m.

Martin's mom and dad had been curious. They would probably check on him a few times. He guessed he should get undressed, get beneath the covers and feign sleep. He'd keep his clothes nearby, neatly folded in case they were discovered. He wasn't well practiced at this sort of thing. He'd been a good kid, even bordering on boring. Eating ice cream away from the kitchen table had been about as wild as it got around the Taylor house, but that had been just fine with him. His dad had always acted as if he were disappointed in Martin, and that had bothered him a lot. Now he understood that his dad had been disappointed in himself. He'd tried to rationalize it by living vicariously through Martin.

Martin surveyed his old bedroom, smiling as his eyes lit on some pages that he'd cut out of hot-rod magazines. He'd always loved cars and motorcycles. In a corner, sat the used chest of drawers his dad had brought home. His mom had later painted it antique white. They had not been well-to-do, but they had gotten by.

He glanced at the window he would use to exit the house and had second thoughts. He had no choice but to go through with it. The window would open easily enough. He'd tried it before. He saw that the screen was off, too. It had come loose in 1990. His dad had never put it back. It would still be there, propped against the house. Martin didn't want to put his parents through this—waking up to find him gone, but there was no other way. He also hoped he could change Stewart's mind. Martin didn't believe the man had always been heartless.

By the time the clock showed 10:00 p.m., the house had grown quiet, but Martin remained in bed another hour just to be sure his parents were asleep. Even then, he hesitated before he quietly climbed out of bed and got dressed. Giving one final look around the room, Martin slid open the window, and crawled out, and dropped to the ground. As he left the yard and stepped onto the sidewalk, everything seemed surreal, and he was reminded of the ghostly world he'd experienced in 2014.

Being in good shape, not in an athletic way but certainly in the sense of having always been on the go, Martin made good time.

Thanks to the aid of a stranger, who Martin had bummed a ride with against his better judgement, he walked through the sliding doors of the Tulsa airport at 3:30 a.m. After checking the information board for the correct gate, he made his way through security and walked to the waiting area near the gate.

Once there, he plopped into a chair. He had about two hours before the flight was to leave. If everything went according to plan, his parents would discover he was gone sometime around 7:30 a.m. By that time, he would be on his way to Williamsburg.

Hearing voices, Martin opened his eyes, and when he saw that it was just after 6:00 a.m., he sat forward. People were already lining up to board the plane. He pushed himself from the chair and went to the bathroom to wash his hands and face. After that, he walked back to the gate. Trying not to be noticed, he kept a comfortable distance. He waited until the area had cleared out and most of the passengers had boarded. Then he strode toward the skywalk.

The lady checking tickets stopped him.

"I left something in the waiting area," he said. "Mom said I could run back and get it, but when I got here, it was gone. It's okay, though. But I need to get back on board, else Mom will come looking for me. Trust me...that won't be good."

The lady smiled. "What was it you lost?"

"A 1957 Chevy Hot Wheel."

"What's your name?" she asked.

Martin almost blurted it out but stopped himself. "Billy," he said, "Billy Smith."

She checked the monitor. "What's your mother's name?"

Martin uttered a silent prayer that someone matching would be on board. "Mary, Mary Smith."

She checked again and then nodded. "All right, Billy. But you'd better hurry. The flight will be leaving in about five minutes."

Thanking the Lord for answering his prayer, Martin scrambled through the skywalk. Once on board, he found an empty seat, sat down, and fastened his seat belt.

Martin was jolted out of a light sleep when the aircraft landed with a thud on the tarmac. It rocked back and forth, rumbling as it slowed, forcing him back against the seat and causing his whole body to vibrate. The idea of being alone made him shiver. His watch showed 8:45 a.m., but that couldn't be right. He'd crossed a time zone, which would put the time at 9:45 a.m. The rally wasn't until tomorrow. He might have been better off to have stayed one more night at home. He just had been too afraid of getting found and of what that might do to his parents.

The plane came to a stop, and everyone started milling around, trying to retrieve their things from the overhead bins.

Martin remained in his seat. Being hosted by his younger self had proven easier than it had with his dad or Krystal. That was to be expected. It was easier to be yourself. The younger Martin had accepted his presence with ease.

After nearly everyone left the plane, Martin got up and walked slowly down the aisle. He exited and went down the skywalk. When he stepped out, the busy airport opened before him, and again, the feeling of being alone threatened to derail his resolve. He took a deep breath. Then he merged with the crowd flowing along the wide concourse, trying to blend in while paying particular attention to the Ground Transportation signs.

When he reached the street level, Martin studied the taxis and buses outside. He would have to stay the night somewhere. His chances of surviving might be better at the airport. He found an area with restaurants and shops. Later, the shaking of his shoulder brought him out of sleep. A man wearing dark glasses stood over him.

"Hey, kid, you've been sitting here for quite a while. Is everything all right?"

Martin sat forward. He'd have to be careful not say the wrong thing and arouse suspicion. "Yeah, I'm okay. I'm not supposed to talk to strangers, though."

"Why don't you come over and sit with me?" the man asked. "Just to be safe."

He didn't look like a cop or security guard.

"Mom got me here early, that's all. Dad will be here any moment. Figured I'd be okay for an hour or so."

The man sat beside Martin. "I'll stay here and keep you company, okay?"

Martin saw a rough looking guy with tattoos coming up the concourse. "I wouldn't do that if I were you."

"Yeah, why's that?"

"Stick around, and you'll find out." Martin held his breath as he waved at the man with tattoos.

When the man waved back, Martin said a silent *thank you*. "Here he comes now. It's going to be fun to watch him rearrange your face."

Without saying another word, the strange man jumped up and darted away.

Martin got up cautiously and strolled through the immediate area.

The man wearing dark glasses was still there, lurking in the distance.

Martin chanced going to the men's room, but when he came out, the man was there, leaning against the wall beside the entrance to the restroom, a smile lifting the corners of his mouth.

"I figured you were bluffing. That man wasn't your daddy. You're here all alone."

"What's it to you?" Martin asked. "And why do you keep following me? What do you want?"

The man pushed away from the wall and moved toward Martin. "Not much," he said, "just a little companionship. It won't hurt a bit. You might even like it. Come on, what do you say?"

"Not a chance, creep. Now beat it before I find a cop."

"You won't call any cops. You're a runaway. You don't want to get caught any more than I do."

Martin turned away and started down the concourse, away from the stranger. He didn't want to get caught, but if staying here with this creep or drawing the attention of the police were his only options, he'd choose the cops. He'd made only a few steps, however, when a hand on his shoulder stopped him and spun him around.

"Not so fast. I'm not through with you just yet," he sneered, grabbing Martin's arm.

Martin struggled to get free, but his young body was no match for the man. "You're messing with the wrong kid, mister. Let me go, else you're going to regret it."

"Oh, I doubt that. On the contrary, I think I'm going to like it very much. What are you going to do, anyway? It doesn't look to me like you got a lot of choice."

Martin decided quickly. It was better to scrub the mission than to end up in the clutches of this loser. He gathered as much strength as he could and let out a yell. "Help! Somebody, help me!"

The man flinched but didn't let go. He shook his head and smiled at the passersby who had slowed their steps to watch the scene unfolding. "Nothing to worry about, just an unruly kid. He's really going to get it when we get home. You can count on that."

Trying again, Martin screamed, "He's not my dad! Just some creep that grabbed me."

A few people stopped and stared, leaning toward one another and talking, but no one did anything.

From behind Martin, someone said, "Hey, mister, ease up. Looks like you're hurting the kid."

"It's none of your business," the man said. "It's between me and my son, so get lost!"

A tall and lanky young man, stepped away from the crowd and came closer. His companions followed.

"Maybe so," the young man said, "but child abuse is against the law, so why don't you just let go of the kid, and everything will be fine."

"He's not my dad!" Martin yelled. "He's just some creep who hangs around the airport, looking for kids like me."

"Shut up!" The creep shouted, shaking Martin.

That's all it took. The young man and several of his friends pulled Martin from the creep's grip and shoved him away.

The lanky young man, who had acted first, said, "I think you're through here, mister. The kid is with us now."

The strange man darted away. If any security personnel had appeared, Martin certainly didn't see any. He hugged his young rescuer. "Thanks, man. You just saved my life."

"Not a problem. The airport is not a safe place for a kid to hang around. Are your parents here? I'll stick around until you find them, if you want."

"That'd be great," Martin said. "Could we talk a minute, just you and me?"

The young man smiled and nodded to his friends. Then he and Martin stepped away from them. "All right. You've got my attention. What's up?"

Martin's mind scrambled for the right approach. "I need your help, but not with finding my parents. That would be a little difficult right now, anyway."

"Why's that? Are you homeless?"

"No, not exactly, but I need to know I can trust you before we go any further."

"Trust me? Trust me with what?"

"I need your help," Martin said. "But I want you to promise me you won't call the police or turn me in right away. Do we have a deal?"

The young man smiled, his expression laced with curiosity and concern. "All right, but at some point, you're going to have to level with me. Trust works both ways." He extended his hand. "Name's Dale, by the way, Dale Carrington. Now, what can I do for you, mister...?"

"Taylor, Martin Taylor. And what I need is transportation."

Dale Carrington's brow drew together, wrinkling his forehead. "Where do you need to go?"

"Can I trust you?"

"You can trust me."

"The College of William and Mary. Do you know where that is?"

Dale smiled and nodded. "Yeah, I know where it is. Question is, why do you need to go there? And why would it be difficult to find your parents?"

Martin nodded. "A political rally is going to be held there today. I need to go to it. And finding my parents would be hard because they are in Tulsa, Oklahoma."

Dale tossed his head in the direction of his friends who were walking down the concourse, and he and Martin started following them. "Tulsa is a long way from Williamsburg," he said. "And it's just my luck that the innocent looking kid I decided to help would turn out to be, let's just say much more than meets the eye. Why would a kid like you want to go to a political rally? You look too young to be interested in politics."

"Someone I need to talk to is going to be there," Martin said.

"Who is it exactly that you need to talk to? Do you have relatives there?"

"His name is Jackson Stewart. I think he's a student. Do you know him?"

"Doesn't ring a bell. "But I know about the rally."

"Could you show me where it is?" Martin asked. "By the way, are you interested in politics?"

"Not so much," Dale said. "I went to one of the rallies. Some of the things they stand for, like helping those less fortunate and easing racial tensions, are good causes. But the way they go about it with all the hate and anger...it's nothing I want to be a part of. And who exactly is Jackson Stewart?"

"It's complicated," Martin said.

Outside the airport, Martin and Dale met up with Dale's friends. After Dale had a private conversation with his companions, everyone loaded onto a shuttle bus that took them to the parking garage. Not long after that, Martin sat in the front seat of a Ford Explorer, between Dale, who drove, and a brown-eyed girl with a pleasant smile.

A few minutes into the rather silent trip, Martin checked his watch. It showed 7:00 a.m., which meant it was 8:00 a.m. in Williamsburg. Martin liked Dale, but he'd also begun to understand what kind of person he was. He would call the police at some point. Martin hoped he'd have a chance to talk with Stewart before that happened. After that, Dale's calling the police would be perfectly fine. Once Martin completed his mission, he would have to get the younger Martin home again. Having assistance from the police would be helpful.

"Are we going to get you there in time?" Dale asked with a touch of humor in his voice.

"Yeah," Martin said. "I can't thank you enough for helping me. I don't know what I would have done if you guys hadn't come along."

Much quicker than Martin thought they would, they arrived at the rally. As it turned out, Dale and his friends were students there.

Dale left to meander through the crowd, and when he returned a few minutes later, He had Jackson Stewart with him.

Well, you got what you wanted, Martin. Now what?

Dale and his friends stepped back to give Martin time alone with Stewart.

"Well," Martin said, "here we are."

Jackson smiled and then took a bite of a half-eaten sandwich. "Yeah, here we are. Now what's this all about? Dale said you were quite adamant about seeing me."

Martin glanced around. He figured Dale had already called the police. "Okay, Jackson. The best way to do this is to just jump in with both feet. Do you believe in time travel?"

A curious look spread across Jackson's face. All right, kid, you look too young to be on drugs or anything like that, so what the heck are you talking about?"

"All right," Martin said. "We've met before, or rather, we will in the future."

"Come on, kid. The future hasn't happened yet."

Martin paused. That was true, but not in this case. "We will meet in 2020, Jackson. And again in 2014. I realize that sounds backward, but that's the way it happens. Except in 2014, I don't think you knew I was there."

"The more you talk, the more I'm convinced you're a nutcase. But you seem awfully intelligent for a kid. You keep looking at my sandwich. Are you hungry?"

Martin hadn't eaten since yesterday. "Yeah," he said, "I am kind of starved."

Jackson took off his backpack and dug out a candy bar. "Here you go, kid. It's all I got. Now what's all this nonsense about us meeting before?"

"We were at a restaurant," Martin said, "only we weren't together."

Martin ripped open the package. It turned out to be a protein bar, but he wasn't particular at the moment. He took a large bite. "I was with my wife, and you were with your brother, McKinley."

Jackson rubbed his forehead, trying to smooth out the wrinkles that had formed there. "So, you know my brother?"

Martin struggled for an answer. The authorities would be there at any moment. "Not really. I was just there and overheard your conversation. You were trying to convince your brother that he and his wife should abort their child."

Jackson's expression hardened. Martin had hit a nerve. "You're talking nonsense, kid. If you can't be coherent, I'm through here. Understand?"

The doctor—at least he would be in the future—was right about one thing. Martin needed to get on with it. "All right. Here it is. You seem like a decent guy right now. I'm even starting to like you. But all of that's going to change in the future. I don't know. Something devastating must have happened to you at some point. Otherwise, you wouldn't have turned out like that."

"What the heck are you trying to say, kid?"

A heavy hand tightened around Martin's shoulder. The authorities had arrived. "It's all about my son, Luke. He means the world to me, Jackson. I'm here to change things so that your animosity toward him might be altered. You will believe you're doing the right thing, but it's wrong, Jackson."

"Are you Martin Taylor?" The man with the heavy hand asked.

"Yes, sir. And I'm glad you're here. I ask only one thing of you. Give me a moment to finish what I've started here."

Martin turned back. "Just remember me, Jackson. Remember what I said."

The policeman, a large but gentle man, led Martin away. "The next time we meet," Martin said, talking to Jackson, "I will give you a keyword—*sandcastle*. Put it to memory."

CHAPTER NINETEEN

Friday, September 13, 1991, 6:00 p.m.

Martin felt about six inches tall as he and his family walked into the living room. The flight back from Williamsburg had been tense and quiet. Now that they were home, Martin suspected the evening would deteriorate, and when his dad dragged a kitchen chair into the room, a knot tightened in his stomach.

Martin's dad planted him in the chair. "All right, young man, this has gone far enough. Do you have any idea of what you just put us through? Your mom is—" He paused and gestured with his hands as if to say, 'See, see what you've done?' "Martin, it's time you learned to consider the consequences of your actions."

Despite his situation, Martin felt a tinge of pride for his father. He might as well have been talking with Grandpa Frank because that was exactly the kind of thing Grandpa would have said. He guessed his father had been listening, after all. Now, as Martin sat there like a suspect in an old Elliot Ness story, sweating beneath the heat of the lights as the minions of justice urged him into spilling the beans, he thought maybe he should come clean. He should tell his parents the truth, no matter how unbelievable that truth might be.

"Okay, Dad. You deserve better than this. You deserve the truth. But let me preface it with a warning."

Preface it? Warning? Come on, Martin. You wouldn't have used words like that when you were this young.

Then again, he wasn't trying to hide anymore, was he? "What you're about to hear," Martin continued, "is going to solidify in your minds that, yes, your son has completely lost his marbles."

Martin's mom and dad exchanged nervous glances.

"Martin," his dad said, "stop stalling and start talking."

Martin shifted in the chair. There was nothing left to do but jump in with both feet. Except he couldn't do that, could he? What had he been thinking?

"Just remember this," he said. "All things are possible through our Father in Heaven."

Martin paused, wondering if he should have said that. Grandpa Frank had been a religious man, but for reasons Martin had never understood, his dad had not followed the same path. Religion was never mentioned in their house. Martin had not been raised in a Christian environment.

Martin waited for an answer. Then, the expression on his dad's face said it all. He was wondering how and when Martin started believing in God.

"How could you possibly know that, Martin?"

Martin recalled sharing his father's thoughts at Grandpa Frank's. "It's called faith, Dad."

His father turned and collapsed onto the sofa. "What did I do, step off into the Twilight Zone?"

Martin knew he'd gone too far. It was time to leave.

"Mom, Dad, I'm sorry for all the problems I caused you through the years, but remember this: I love you with all of my heart."

Martin closed his eyes and prayed. Then an image appeared—words written like clouds in the sky—displaying the date, December 20, 1999.

• • •

Martin adjusted to the time shift. He had jumped into the mind of sixteen-year-old Martin Taylor. He was driving Grandpa's GTO. Martin erected the protective barrier, leaving enough room for the younger Martin to think on his own. A powerful car was no place to have your concentration compromised.

Martin's dad had never understood why Grandpa Frank had bypassed him and given Martin his watch. But it was the GTO Grandpa had given to Martin on his sixteenth birthday that solidified the barrier between Martin and his dad.

The first thing Martin always did while visiting Grandpa was go to the garage to admire the classic ride. Martin downshifted the old Pontiac and introduced himself to the teenage Martin as 'the random thoughts' responsible for sending eight-year-old Martin to Williamsburg. Sixteen-year-old Martin was more willing to accept such a concept, though not so eager to take a backseat to the older, more experienced version. Martin reassured his host that the visit would be temporary. He also informed him that he was there to revisit Jackson Stewart. Skirting the issue was not an option. Martin would have to rise above his self-doubt and face the encounter head on. He was a traveler now, and God had blessed him with this unusual ability for a reason.

Martin suggested that they go to the library for a little espionage. The younger Martin protested but only because the excursion would interrupt his driving.

Martin found the telephone number for Jackson Stewart by using the library's computer. After that, he drove to Woodward Park, parked beside the rose garden, and called the doctor.

When Stewart answered, Martin almost lost his nerve. "Could I speak to Doctor Stewart, please?"

"I'm sorry," a young woman said. "The doctor is presently seeing patients and won't be available until later. Is this an emergency?"

"Not exactly," Martin said, "but it's extremely important I speak with him. If I leave my number, will you have him call me back as soon as possible?"

"I'll inform the doctor, but he's busy. It might take him awhile to return the call. Are you a patient?"

"No," Martin said, "just an old friend. Tell him Martin Taylor is in town and wants to talk about sandcastles."

After a long pause, the receptionist asked, "Sandcastles?"

"That's right. He will know what it means."

Martin ended the call. The thought of meeting with Stewart left a knot in his stomach. Knowing that, only a few days ago, he had worried about what to get Susan and Luke for their birthdays, intensified the sensation.

In the silence of the nearly empty park, an elderly couple walked past the car. Their togetherness reminded Martin of the special bond he and Susan shared, and tears leaked from the corners of his eyes. He longed to be with her right now. Then, he became aware that his emotional state of mind was arousing young Martin's curiosity. He quickly shifted his thoughts to the phone call he hoped to receive from Stewart. Martin wondered about John Rainbow and what his fellow traveler might think of Martin's meeting with Stewart.

The sound of the old Nokia cell phone startled Martin, bringing him back to the moment. It was Doctor Stewart.

"Who the hell are you?" the voice demanded.

Martin didn't know what to say. He wondered what John Rainbow would do. He would tell Martin to go home and stop meddling. But Martin could not do that.

"I think you know," Martin said. "At the College of William and Mary, you gave me something to eat. I don't know if I thanked you for that or not. It was an act of kindness. You were a good person. What happened?"

"Well, now it's my turn to say *I think you know*. You told me back in 1991 that something bad was going to happen. Less than a year later, a lunatic lumbered into my parents' home and slaughtered them. Now, how could you possibly have known that unless you had something to do with it?"

Martin squeezed the phone. He hadn't actually *known* that. It had been nothing more than an educated guess.

"You're a psychologist," he said. "I was simply doing my own version of that. Now I hope to talk some sense into you."

"My father was interested in time travel," Stewart said. "Why don't you and I get together and discuss this? Perhaps you could stop by my office today."

An awareness of someone lurking nearby crawled up Martin's spine. He didn't see anyone. "All right," he said. "But not in your office. I'll meet you in a public place."

"Do you mistrust people in general, or are doctors more specific to your condition?"

"It's complicated. "It pays to be careful. That's all." Martin realized immediately that his choice of words might be taken as an indication of paranoia by a psychologist.

"All right, Martin. I'll humor you and agree to your conditions but only because my curiosity outweighs my better judgment. Give me the particulars of where and when, and I'll do my best to be there."

Again, a feeling of being watched came over Martin, similar to the sensation he'd experienced at the cemetery where Candy Barnes was buried and at the hospital where he'd met John Rainbow.

"I'm sure you know where Woodward Park is."

"Yes, of course. Is that the place?"

"I'll be in the parking lot, sitting alone in a white GTO with a black convertible top, vintage car. You can't miss it."

"All right, Martin. It might take a while, so don't give up on me. I'll pull up beside you and wave."

Not long after Martin had disconnected, a car pulled up beside him, and the passenger waved.

Martin checked his watch, nodded, and climbed out of the car, leaning against the GTO as an older version of Stewart approached.

"Nice ride," Jackson said. "You've grown since our last meeting."

Grandpa Frank surprised me with it on my sixteenth birthday. I hope to pass it along to Luke someday. But you will want to change that, take the law into your own hands."

"Why are you so concerned about me and your son. You've got me all wrong. I've dedicated my life to helping people with mental disorders, not hurting them."

"I want to believe that," Martin said, "but I know what happens in 2020. And it isn't good."

Stewart looked away, gazing at the scenery, his expression intense.

Martin paused, struggling to cope with such an unbelievable and horrifying concept.

"You are more delusional than I thought, Martin. I've never harmed anyone in my life."

"I believe that of you now, but things will change."

"Try to be a bit more specific, my old friend."

"I'm talking about time travel, Doctor Stewart. You will convince yourself that going back and preventing the birth of someone like, Luke is not the same as murder."

A curious expression crawled across Doctor Stewart's face.

"You paint a dismal picture of my future, Martin. How many times do I have to tell you that my life's work is designed around helping people, not harming them?"

"And I'm sure you have. But I encourage you to look into the background of the man who attacked your parents."

Stewart sighed and looked down before offering a guarded smile. "Like you, I admire vintage cars. I keep a '68 Mustang garaged. Occasionally, I take it out for a spin. Mind if I take a look?"

Stewart slid into the passenger seat, a wide grin spreading across his face. "Man, this is nice. Love the black leather. Someone did a bang-up job on the restoration."

"My grandfather had it done. Every time I drive it, I fall in love again."

As Stewart climbed out of the car, he said, "I know what you mean." He hesitated. "What about this time-travel thing? My father was really into it, kept extensive notes, which I inherited. Psychology was my mom's idea. My father believed traveling through time was possible, but I don't think I ever really believed it, not until now."

A familiar chill ran up Martin's spine. Another traveler had just arrived.

"How you do you accomplish it?" Stewart asked. "How did you establish an electromagnetic envelope stable and strong enough to do the job?"

Martin was beginning to like Doctor Stewart, but this was not the time for chit-chat. "I didn't have to," he said, his speech accelerating with his pulse. "I think about it, and it happens. We need to get out of here, Jackson!"

"What on earth are you talking about?"

"Another traveler has found us. There's no time to explain."

As they jumped into the GTO, an old Ford station wagon whipped behind them and stopped, blocking their exit.

In the rearview mirror, Martin glimpsed the traveler.

Then, the other version of Doctor Stewart got out of his station wagon and walked over, a crooked smile turning the corners of his mouth.

"Hello, Martin," he said. "Tag, you're it. The game is over."

While the nice Stewart sat in the passenger's seat with his mouth hanging open, distant memories flooded Martin's mind. Something similar to this had happened before. He'd been trapped at school when a group of kids cornered him, beating the daylights out of him.

"Don't look so shocked," the other Doctor Stewart said. "Funny how things work out, isn't it? He paused, a far-off look in his eyes. "Now, let's get down to business."

A bead of sweat slid down Martin's back. How was he going to get out of this?

The other Stewart grinned. "You've created a lot of loose ends, my old friend." He unbuttoned his jacket and reached beneath it, and when he brought his hand back out, it held a hypodermic needle. "Nothing to worry about. This will put you to sleep, and when you wake up, I'll be gone.

The reality of the situation settled over Martin. His heart raced. He snatched the keys from the GTO and bolted for 21st Street, which bordered the northern end of the park.

The nice Stewart followed.

When they reached 21st Street, Martin and Stewart ran toward Peoria Avenue.

Upon seeing a cop, Martin jumped up and down to flag him down. Then, he closed his eyes and left that time and place. He had no idea of how the meeting of the younger and older Stewart would play out, if it were to happen. He hadn't considered the possibility of two versions of the same person existing at the same time. Perhaps the arrival of the police officer would scare the older Stewart away.

CHAPTER TWENTY

Sunday, May 04, 2014

Friday, September 15, 1978

It had been an easy decision for Martin to revisit the shadowy world of 2014. As soon as he gained his bearings, he ran into the office and switched on the computer. He and Tanner McIntosh had talked about some unusual things. Martin punched in *Camp Hero*. Something about his meeting with two different Stewarts didn't add up. If Stewart was a traveler, he would have known what Martin had been up to at the park. Stewart could not exist in duality. The answer suddenly occurred to Martin. As John Rainbow had been trying to tell him, each time he jumped, he created new fragments. Each carried its own reality.

The search term *Camp Hero* brought up *The Philadelphia Experiment*. Martin followed the links and read every article he could find.

● ● ●

Martin stood in the foyer of Grandpa Frank's house, in the mind of his father, young Billy Taylor. As before, Grandpa acknowledged the presence of his son.

"Sorry to disturb you," Martin said, "but we need to discuss this further."

Grandpa Frank put his work aside. "All right, Billy."

"It's complicated, Grandpa. I'm not sure where to begin."

Grandpa Frank leaned back in his chair and picked up the cigar smoldering in the ashtray. "Since when did you start calling me *Grandpa*?"

The intensity of the moment threatened to steal Martin's nerve. He'd gone out on a limb, and now there were only two things he could do: Turn tail and run or gather his courage and do what he'd come here to do. "I'm going to tell you something that will either convince you that I've lost my mind or fill you with curiosity."

"Well, you've piqued my interest, for sure. Go on."

"In 1964 you purchased a GTO."

"We talked about this, Billy. I will get you a car on your sixteenth birthday, but it will not be the GTO. And why did you bring up the year?"

Martin shook his head. "You're still not grasping the situation, Grandpa. Maybe this will help. My memories of the car began when you had it stored in the garage. You will make that decision in 1990. We had heart-to-heart talks. While sitting in the car, you asked if I believed in time travel."

Martin's Grandfather placed the cigar in the ashtray.

"Time travel is a reality, Grandpa. Five years from now, your son will have a son. He will name him after you. It's me, Grandpa, your grandson, Martin."

"Good God in Heaven," Grandpa said. He laid his hand across his forehead. "What about Billy? What's this doing to him?"

"He's fine," Martin said. "I've learned to mask my presence just as a child dropped into water knows not to breathe until they surface. Once I started traveling, all the strange conversations we had made sense. They piqued my interest, compelled me dig deeper. What I found is intriguing but frightening."

Martin's grandfather waited patiently, a look somewhere between anxiety and longing-to know coming across his face.

"My traveling landed me onboard the U.S.S. Eldridge, part of the Philadelphia Experiment a secret, government project concerning the concept of rendering battleships invisible. Once there, I entered the mind of Clayton Devereaux, a gunner on board the Eldridge. My mother's maiden name was Devereaux."

Grandpa smiled. "Billy managed to do one thing right." He paused. "I guess our conversations in the garage, Martin, weren't just the ramblings of an old man, after all."

"You told me you traveled just by thinking about it," Martin said. "That's exactly how I do it." He considered his words. "We're both tangled up in this, Grandpa. You were born on August 12, 1943, the date of the original Philadelphia Experiment. The government succeeded in rendering the Eldridge invisible, all right, but they inadvertently teleported the ship to another location. It came back a disaster—crew members altered, mentally and physically."

Grandpa Frank fumbled his cigar and almost dropped it. Regathering his composure, he said, "Go on."

"Forty years later," Martin said, "on August 12, 1983, my birthday, the government's meddling interlocked the Eldridge between the two time periods, which tore a hole in hyperspace, making travel once again possible. The two crewmembers who'd jumped from the Eldridge and landed in 1983, then went back to 1943 and shut down the generators, collapsing the hole in hyperspace."

Grandpa Frank nervously drew on his cigar and then said, "Where is all of this leading, Martin?"

Martin paused and then continued. "In 2020, which is my real time, controversial abortion legislation will be proposed by powerful politicians. My son, Luke, your great grandson, will be instrumental in stopping the action. But not if I can fix things—repair the hole that's been reopened in hyperspace—then these events won't occur, and everything will revert to the way it was before. My correct handling of the situation is crucial. These politicians will be determined. A powerful doctor they are associated with plans to travel back in time and prevent Luke from being born, a devious form of murder."

Grandpa Frank sat forward in his chair. "God in Heaven, Martin. He pushed his hair back then smoothed it into place. "So, you're saying you're not the only traveler involved with this?"

Martin offered a nervous smile. "To the best of my knowledge, there are only three of us, though my traveling technique is different from the method used by the others."

Grandpa Frank drew in smoke from his cigar and puffed out a bluish cloud. "How is it, different?"

"My age changes according to the date, and I remain myself as time permits. If not, I go into the minds of relatives."

Grandpa nodded. "That explains how you're able to be here." He paused. "And these other travelers plan to go after Luke?"

"One of them does, a psychologist named Stewart."

"You've narrowed it down to one. Will finding him be difficult?"

"Finding him is not the problem. It's stopping him. I don't know if I have what it takes."

Martin's grandfather blew out another cloud, letting it hang in the air. "Didn't we already have a conversation concerning your lack of self-confidence?"

"Yes. But my actions must be executed perfectly. Otherwise, everything could backfire, causing the hyperspace anomaly to grow. God only knows what might happen after that."

"I understand. But doing nothing is not an option."

"You're right, Grandpa. I wish I were more like you, taking problems head-on without hesitation."

He smiled. "You are, Martin. You just haven't accepted it. True confidence comes from knowing God and following a path that pleases him." Martin's grandfather stared into space for a moment. Then asked, "How old is Luke, in your world?"

"He just turned seventeen. He's a good person. You would like him."

"I already do, Martin. The best way to face any adversary is on a level playing field. You level the field with knowledge, learning as much as you can about your opponent, their strengths and weaknesses. You said that your traveling technique is different. Use that to your advantage."

"Of course," Martin said. "The other travelers travel as themselves, no matter how far back or forward they go. They can't exist in both time periods."

But Doctor Stewart managed to appear in duality within the same time period, didn't he Martin?

A noise coming from outside the house drew Martin's attention. Through the slightly imperfect glass of the Tudor-style office window, he saw Grandma Phyllis tending the flowerbeds.

"I've already gone back," Martin continued, "and met with Doctor Stewart—except he was known as Jackson Stewart then—as my nine-year-old self. I don't think he would have recognized me had I not told him who I was."

"Why did you give away your edge so easily?"

"I thought I could reason with him before he became jaded. I almost succeeded. Stewart has some good qualities. They just keep getting overridden by the dark side of his nature."

"Unfortunately, that is the typical human condition," Grandpa said. "Without God in our lives, we are all at the mercy of our own desires. You've got this, Martin."

"It's not that simple, Grandpa. "For instance, how much damage have I done just by coming here. It will, no doubt, have an effect. You'll do things differently, make decisions that you otherwise wouldn't have. I love you, Grandpa. I don't want to do anything that might cause you harm."

A tear formed in Grandpa Frank's eye and ran crookedly down his cheek. "Martin, you've brought me great joy today. I now know I have a wise and thoughtful grandson and a wonderful great grandson."

"Thanks, Grandpa, but I will never be half the man you are."

"Oh, I wouldn't say that. From where I'm sitting, you sound like you're quite the man already. Your behavior and the things you've said have made me enormously proud. Now, let's get back to the problem at hand, that of saving my great grandson. Even though you've tipped your hand with the age thing, you still have the element of surprise on your side. For example, you could inhabit a relative who doesn't resemble you and create a tremendous advantage."

"Sounds easy enough."

"I have faith in you, Martin. You can, and must, do this."

"Thanks. However, the problem will be determining how far back to go. I could concentrate only on my family and on saving Luke, but I can't do that. Other people are involved. Luke has a friend, Candy. Doctor Stewart went back, caused her to be stillborn. God only knows what Stewart has set in motion and what the damage will be. The question is, at what point do I inadvertently cross the line—stop being the good guy and start being the villain in someone else's world?"

Concern wrinkled Grandpa's face. "I suggest you take it to the Lord in prayer, Martin. God gifted you with this power. He will guide you in how to use it."

CHAPTER TWENTY-ONE

Saturday, May 02, 2020, 11:30 a.m.

Martin floated in darkness; the void in between timelines, quieter than before, missing the crackling electrical field. Even before leaving Grandpa Frank's time and place, Martin had considered his next move. Doctor Stewart's elimination of Candy Barnes would have occurred near Luke's appointment on May 04, 2020, when everything started. Keeping that in mind, Martin formed the date of May 02, 2020, in his mind, and instantaneously, the fabric of his world in 2020 materialized.

He was driving the Audi, heading east on Highway 412. He had no idea why or where he was going. The first chance he got, he pulled off the road and turned back, going west toward Tulsa. Thirty minutes later, Martin pulled off the highway and into the parking lot outside the office of Doctor Stewart. Being Saturday, the office would be closed, but Martin saw Stewart's black BMW parked near the back. The doctor was in.

Martin leaned back in the seat and waited. Sooner or later, Stewart would come out of the office and go wherever he needed to go to accomplish his mission. Martin would follow him.

Stewart had chosen this day to travel back to May 17, 1995, to make an attempt on the life of Candy Barnes. All Martin had to do was find out how Stewart accomplished the trip back in time and stop him.

This time, Martin would not slink into a corner, hoping someone else would take care of everything. This problem had been placed on his shoulders by design, and only he could solve it.

Martin sat forward. Stewart had finally come out of the building. As the doctor exited the lot, Martin followed, keeping distance between them.

Stewart took the Utica exit off the expressway and then followed the feeder road past the stop sign and through the intersection. Passing Utica, the doctor continued north along Peoria Avenue, stopping a few miles from town, near a dilapidated industrial area.

The street sign had been torn down. No attempt had been made by the city to replace the marker. It wasn't hard to understand why. Weeds nearly obscured the chain-link fence surrounding the site that occupied most of the block on the north side of the street. It wasn't just the fenced-off site that appeared abandoned. The entire area looked deserted. Martin found the concept frightening but intriguing. He'd always been fascinated by unused areas that continued to exist in their own little worlds. Then again, his father had often told him that he lived in his own little world. Perhaps that's why he found such things as defunct, one-time bustling businesses interesting. He loved contemplating the mystery behind why the concerns had ended up that way.

Martin snapped back to his senses as Stewart's BMW glided across the weed-choked parking lot toward a metal building the size of two football fields. Stewart had somehow gotten beyond the fence and gained access to the area. If Stewart wanted to conceal his actions, this was a good place to do it.

A few hundred feet away, Martin found the gate where Stewart had entered. It was locked but not by padlock. It had been electronically secured, which meant Stewart had been here before.

Thoughts of turning around and leaving ran through Martin, but there had to be a way to get inside the fence other than climbing over it. Even if he could physically scale it, being suspended during the climb would leave him exposed. As odd as it seemed, there were no tears, rips, or holes in the galvanized fence. The thought of the barrier being maintained gave Martin even more reason to worry. Everyone else apparently avoided the area.

Martin hesitated. Then he grabbed a handful of wire and hoisted himself up. Reaching the top, he threw both legs over and lowered himself to the crumbling tarmac on the other side. Hoping he hadn't been detected, he scurried across the lot toward the entrance to the building—a large metal door.

The door creaked open, its rusty hinges announcing Martin's intrusion. Holding the door, he stared inside.

Okay, Martin, here you are. Now what?

Machinery occupied the expanse, idle but ready to go, or so it appeared—left behind, still arranged to manufacture whatever had been the product of such a business.

Martin stepped inside. Easing the door shut, he cautiously walked into the expanse, his shoes crunching like gunshots in the silence. From somewhere below, a distinctive electrical hum charged the air. Martin's throat tightened. Such a disturbance did not belong in the forgotten building. As he adjusted to the darkness, a substructure along the east side, a cinderblock wall with a door in the center, caught his attention. He crept forward and eased it open, peering into a stairwell that led downward into a spiraling darkness. The electrical hum was much louder there.

Then, another problem grabbed Martin's attention. He spun around.

A pack of dogs that showed no sign of being intimidated stared him down, their pearly-white teeth dripping with saliva.

Martin bolted into the stairwell and slammed the door. He'd either have to wait there until the dogs lost interest or follow the stairs down to wherever they led. Or feel his way down. Darkness surrounded him. An idea blossomed in his mind. His phone. It might just be there. He drove his hand into his pocket. The phone didn't have a flashlight app, but the light from the screen would be enough. He found it, shined it toward his feet, and carefully descended the stairs. The thought of meeting Stewart wasn't much more appealing than facing the dogs, but what other choice did he have?

The door at the bottom of the stairs creaked open.

Martin sucked in a breath as pins and needles of anxiety burned within his chest and arms. He crammed the phone into his pocket and flattened himself against the wall, his heart pounding.

It was Stewart!

Apparently lost in thought, the doctor rushed past.

Martin closed his eyes and slowly released his breath. Then he slipped through the door into the basement. If the dogs were still upstairs, Stewart would have to deal with them, which should keep him occupied.

In one sweep, Martin took in his surroundings, a twenty-five-hundred-square-foot room packed with wires, transformers, computers, and a massive coil of wire surrounding an oval-shaped patch of pulsating light. Doctor Stewart's time machine.

Disable it, Martin! Do it now!

A bank of monitors made up the control panel. Martin found a swivel chair and rolled it to a keyboard. Completely wiping the hard drive would be ideal, but any kind of damage might disrupt the machine. He clicked on File Explorer. An array of files flashed up. Nothing as obvious as *time travel*, but one labeled *electromagnetics* looked promising.

Martin double-clicked the file, hit Delete, and the monitors began to flicker. Behind him, the pulsating intensified, and the humming grew louder. Whatever he'd done didn't seem to agree with the equipment. A bead of sweat slid down his back. He backed away from the coil and then spun around.

The basement door was still closed.

Stewart had yet to come back into the room. The disturbance should have drawn his attention.

Martin Strode to the door and eased it open, a multitude of fears racing through him. Where was Stewart? What effect would all of this have on Susan and Luke?

Pushing those thoughts aside, Martin bounded up the stairs and threw the door open. Instead of finding an escape route, he stared into the distorted face of Doctor Stewart.

Martin's vision blurred as he struggled to process his next move. He shifted his weight and prepared to shove Stewart aside.

The element of surprise giving him momentum, Stewart resisted. He pushed Martin down the stairs and forced him into the basement. He didn't stop there but continued to push and shove.

Martin tumbled into the pulsating light, fighting to maintain control. For the first time, he floated in the darkness of the time tunnel against his own will. Doctor Stewart, with the aid of his time machine had seen to that. A tornado-like roar filled the expanse while blasts of lightning flashed in the distance.

Martin's mind raced for answers, images of various times and places streaking through him like an out-of-control kaleidoscope. He had been traveling in his own way, but now he was speeding through time in a sort of cosmic double jeopardy that would surely carry dangerous consequences.

Instinctively, Martin pulled his thoughts away from fear and panic and conjured a calendar in his mind, but with no clear path of where to go, the imaginary pages rifled past as if caught in a windstorm. In his mind, he thrust his hand forward, grabbed one of the moving pages, and brought it to his forehead.

An ear-shattering boom, like that of a fighter jet bursting through the sound barrier, resonated through Martin, and he opened his eyes to the semi-dark interior of a public bus. He glanced to his right. Across the aisle, a lady smiled.

Martin glanced at his watch. It showed, Monday, September 02. He fished his phone from his pocket, which indicated the year to be 2019.

A few hours later, the bus rumbled to a stop. It had been a long ride. Martin scrambled from the seat and started down the aisle, wondering if he might have luggage. As he stepped off the bus, he checked his reflection in the mirror. It wasn't a younger or an older version of Martin Taylor who stared back at him but the same one who had gone into the basement of the building at the defunct industrial site.

As Martin followed the small crowd of passengers to a nearby restaurant, he recognized the area. He'd stepped off the bus into Panama City, Florida.

He checked his watch. It showed 10:00 a.m. In approximately one hour, the 2019 version of Martin Taylor would walk away from the pool area at Marathon Resort, where he and his family were staying, and go to the beach. It was the vacation in which he and Luke had failed to finish the sandcastle. Someone had been watching them, and that had made Martin nervous. The question was: If he, the now Martin Taylor, also showed up at the beach, what would happen?

The lady who had been sitting across the aisle on the bus walked over. "You look a little lost," she said. "I'm going inside to get something to eat. Would you like to join me?"

Martin thought about it. He had an hour to wait, and he was hungry. "Sure, that'd be nice."

They walked through the front door, partially blocked by an *A*-shaped chalkboard with pink words scribbled across it.

Once they were inside and seated, the lady said, "Name's Laura. I've never been to Florida, so I thought I'd come down and see what all the fuss is about. How about you? Are you here for business or pleasure?"

"A little of both," Martin said.

Actually, he thought, *I'm here in duplicate—two of us for the price of one.*

She smiled. "Forgive me for being presumptuous, even a little weird, but I don't remember seeing you get on the bus. It was almost like you just sort of popped in."

Martin shook his head, but that was what had happened. Had others on the bus noticed? He had checked his watch and phone, but he'd also stumbled through a magnetic bubble. His devices could be wrong. "Could you tell me what the date is?" he asked.

She looked away for a moment, and when she turned back, she said, "Just my luck. I finally find a nice-looking guy who is easy to talk to, and he turns out to be a nutcase. It's Monday, the second of September. Why would you not know that? And how did you get on that bus?"

Martin ignored the questions. "What year is it?"

She shook her head. "Good Lord, hon. What's your name, anyway? I forgot to ask."

"You can call me Martin."

"Well, Martin, you really are a basket case, aren't you? It's 2019, hon. Do you even know where you are?"

Martin grinned. He was starting to like Laura in an odd sort of way. "Panama City," he said, "in the middle of seafood country, but this place makes a mean cheeseburger."

"Cheeseburgers, huh? I like that." She paused. "I kind of like you, too. Don't get me wrong. I'm not exactly desperate. Just a bit disillusioned, you know. A sort of midlife crisis, I guess."

"Don't worry about it," Martin said. "I'm on the run myself. Except what you're running away from, I'm trying to find." A warm breeze blew salty air through the restaurant. Martin checked his hand for his wedding band. It wasn't there. He had no idea why. "I'm married, though. I don't want to compromise a good thing. My occupation requires me to travel...in some unusual ways."

Laura rolled her eyes. "Let me guess. You're some kind of spy or undercover agent, right?"

"You could say that."

Laura studied Martin's face. Then she pushed away from the table. "I need to freshen up. I'll be back."

As soon as Laura ducked into the lady's room, Martin searched for his wallet. He breathed a sigh of relief when he found it in his pants pocket, holding some cash and a few credit cards. He tossed a twenty on the table and left before Laura could return. He didn't like ditching her. After all, she was a like-minded soul in terms of her confused state of mind. But it was best this way.

Outside, Martin waved down a cab and climbed in. Later, he stood outside the Marathon Resort. The doors leading into the resort loomed a few yards ahead. Continuing, Martin cautiously stepped inside and walked across the marble floors to the front desk.

"Good afternoon," the clerk said. "Do you have a reservation?"

"No. But I'm thinking about it. Would it be all right if I checked out the pool area?"

"Of course. But someone will need to go with you. It's policy. I could arrange for a short tour."

Martin thought for a moment. No doubt he resembled a vagrant in his current condition. The resort was used to dealing with such things—unwanted people coming in off the street. He considered handing the clerk one of his credit cards but thought better of it. Martin Taylor and family would already be checked in. "Let me give it some thought," he said.

Outside, Martin found an area where he could access the beach. He'd have to be careful to get there unnoticed and blend in. Cautiously, he climbed an out-of-the-way sandy dune choked with seagrass, made his way down, and stepped onto the beach.

Immediately, Martin paused, totally unprepared for what he saw— Susan and Luke coming from the hotel. The other Martin was there, too— the one who belonged in this time and place.

It was the most disturbing thing Martin had ever witnessed, but things were about to get worse. Doctor Stewart lurked in the distance.

Stewart remained motionless, then slowly made his way toward the bizarre family reunion, never missing a beat as he pulled a pistol from his pocket and screwed on a silencer with practiced precision.

Martin's throat clenched. He forced himself to continue, closing in from the east as his nemesis came from the west, though his disbelief suddenly melted as Susan brought reality to this scene.

With tears streaming down her face, she glanced back and forth, between past and present, uttering one word. "Martin?"

Standing beside a partially-built sandcastle, Luke followed his mother's lead.

Ignoring them, Stewart shoved the gun into Martin's side. "Shocking, isn't it, meeting yourself face to face? No matter how many times I experience it, I can't get used to it. As jaded as you think I've become, Martin, I'd rather not have to kill you in front of your family. Turn around and start walking."

Martin smiled at Susan, straightening his posture, and began walking. At some point, he would turn the tables on Stewart, make the pathetic wimp pay for all of this. But for now, he would play along. Getting the lunatic away from his family would be a good idea.

A few miles up the beach, Stewart coaxed Martin north, guiding him along the same path Martin had taken earlier, a grassy area between two restaurants, which was about as unpopulated as you could get near the beach in Panama City.

Martin glanced at the weapon gouging his side. "You don't have to do this. I'll do anything you ask. Just don't harm my family, okay?"

"Sorry, Martin. No can do." He shook his head. "Our relationship just isn't working out, my old friend."

Waves crashing against the shoreline—quiet enough to soothe but loud enough to mask unwanted annoyances—caught Martin's attention. His captor held the pistol loosely, confident to the point of being cocky, even careless.

Do it, Martin!"

As if he'd known what was coming, Stewart jumped back, brought the weapon up, and fired.

CHAPTER TWENTY-TWO

A current time and place in a parallel universe

Small, puffy clouds dotted one of the most intense blue skies John had ever seen, but it was tainted by a bank of darkness sitting along the western horizon, an approaching storm that had greatly reduced the number of people on the beach. He ambled along the water's edge, following Sylvia who would stop occasionally to examine a shell the surf had dragged in.

She held one out and smiled. "Look at this one."

To John, the pink-colored shells all looked pretty much the same, but he lovingly held it, feigning amazement. He couldn't think of anything that made him as happy as walking with Sylvia, but tonight, a restless feeling threatened not only their serene jaunt along the sand but also the whole of what had been their peaceful world for the last few days. Several people still walked the area, though one in particular, had drawn John's attention.

Ever since his return to Sylvia, their daily walks had put joy in John's heart. In this time and place, the madness of traveling could almost be forgotten.

The strange man continued steadily toward them. Something about his being there was all wrong. Keeping a distance of about twenty yards, he paused, the wind blowing his hair across his face, as he signaled for John to come closer.

John honored the man's request and then said, "you look a little lost. Is there something I can do for you?"

"Are you John?"

John glanced back at Sylvia. She was busy studying another shell and hadn't fully taken notice of his interaction with the stranger. "Do I know you?"

"Andrew sent me. I don't have much time. He made sure of that, an act of nervousness on his part, for which I am more grateful than he knows. The time disturbances have escalated to previously unknown levels. Andrew said you would understand. It's bad, John. The continuum is being ripped to shreds. Everyone feels it, people on the street even. They don't know what it is, just that something's not right."

"How did you find me?" John asked, though he already knew the answer.

"I had nothing to do with it. It was all Andrew. That he would take such measures indicates the seriousness of this matter."

The stranger tipped an imaginary hat. Then turned and walked away.

Reluctantly, John trudged back to Sylvia, who still searched for shells she had yet to discover.

The nervous agent would soon be gone. Andrew had persuaded him to come here. No one wanted to travel, not even Andrew. The whole department depended on John to do it for them. As if to dot the *i*, the darkness sitting on the horizon would not let John forget that. The storm had been building for days.

Sylvia smiled, the ocean breeze whipping her blondish-grey hair about in unmanageable ways.

"Have I told you how much I love you?" John asked.

"Yes. But only two times today. You're behind schedule."

John pulled her close, stroked her hair, her face, and then gave her a soft kiss. "You are my world, Sylvia."

"Something's wrong, isn't it?"

The surf crashed in, closer than before, misting their faces with sea spray. "It's the darkness on the horizon," John said.

"A storm," she said. "A bad one from the looks of it, but nothing we haven't seen before."

"I'm afraid it is, my dear. And only the beginning of what will continue to get worse."

"You're going away again, aren't you?"

John looked into Sylvia's eyes, wishing he could soften the bluntness of the situation. "These few days have been the happiest of my life. I wish there were another way."

"Maybe there is. We'll figure it out. If nothing else, just stay one more night."

Another wave came in with more force than before, drenching them with salty water.

"Nothing would make me happier, but we don't have that much time. I saw it coming. I just didn't want to let myself believe it. As much as I wish it weren't so, my being here is destroying your world; my absence from mine is leaving the continuum at the mercy of those who could unknowingly unravel it." He shook his head. "Of all the people involved in this quagmire, I should understand enough to explain it to you, but the truth is, I don't. I still have trouble accepting that it's real—that you and I are standing here on the beach, and all of those other worlds are out there."

Wrinkles creased her forehead. "Like Venus and Mars?"

"Sort of." John said. "But more like reflections in a mirror. We accept the refection as our own, as long as it behaves the way we expect it to, but what would happen if our reflections didn't behave as we expect them to?"

"I guess that would be a little unnerving."

"To take the analogy a step further," John continued, "how would you feel if your reflection stepped through to your side of the mirror?"

She didn't answer, just stared at John with longing eyes.

"That's what I've done, Sylvia. I've broken the rules and stepped through the mirror into your world. I shouldn't have done that."

Tears leaked from her eyes and rolled down her face. "I've something to confess, John. I remember being in your world, too. I thought I was crazy, that I was losing my mind."

John shook his head. "To make matters worse, there are people out there who do understand, or at least they think they do. I have to stop them, try to put everything back in order. It's what I do. It's not right for me to turn my back on those who trust me. I'm constantly torn between my sense of duty, and my wanting to be with you."

John let go of Sylvia. He looked into her eyes once last time. Then he turned and walked away.

He heard her calling after him but continued on.

Suddenly, she caught him from behind and spun him around. Wrapping her arms around him, she pulled him close, pressing her wet body against his. "I love you."

Tears streamed down John's face as he resisted an urge to remain there with Sylvia. But his decision had already been made. Grasping her arms, he allowed himself to feel their warmth for a split second. Then he pulled himself away, dropped his hands, and left her.

For a while Sylvia's soft voice, called after him but soon faded, swallowed by the rising tide.

John kept walking. He would never return.

CHAPTER TWENTY-THREE

Aboard the U.S.S. Eldridge
Thursday, August 12, 1943

Martin opened his eyes to find himself in another world. The small enclosure with metal flooring pitched and rolled, leaving no time to adjust to the effects of travel. He immediately began to assess the situation.

Once again, Stewart had tried to kill him, acting with no more concern than if he'd been swatting a fly.

A grease-smeared young man walked over and stared down at Martin. "What the hell are you doing here, sailor?"

Martin sat up, though a brief spout of dizziness slowed the action. "I don't know. Where am I?"

The young man rolled his eyes and shook his head. "Where in hell do you think you are?"

Martin got to his feet and glanced around. "Inside an old ship of some kind, I'd say."

"Old, Ship?" the young man said, "you're in the engine room of a practically new Cannon-class destroyer escort, goofball. She runs better than anything I've ever been on." The young man paused. "Speaking of age, you look too old to be a sailor. And you ain't no officer, else I'd remember your face. I make it a point to do that. It's just good thinking. You're dressed funny, too. Maybe you ought to start explaining yourself. The Germans have spies, you know. Maybe you're one of them."

The young man's words caused Martin to remember some details he'd run across while researching the matter. His ending up here, on board the U.S.S Eldridge, followed a twisted logic. He didn't want to add to the confusion, but he needed to confirm his suspicions. Gathering his courage, he asked, "Could you tell me what year it is?"

"For crying out loud, you're in worse shape than I thought. It's 1943."

"August 12, 1943?" Martin asked to confirm that his hearing was sound.

"That's right. Now you're coming around. Maybe there's hope for you, after all. Before we get all chummy, though, maybe you ought to tell me just who in the heck you are and what you're doing here."

Martin scanned the engine room. Two more mechanics or crew members were busy checking equipment. "The name is Martin Taylor."

"Okay, Martin Taylor, now for the big one. *Why* are you here?"

The question put a knot in Martin's stomach. Had his attempt to derail Doctor Stewart backfired? Was he now traveling to times and places locked into the programming of Stewart's machine, with no control of his own? And what would happen to him if he were on board the Eldridge when the ship went through the experiment that would ultimately send it into hyperspace?

Martin scanned the name displayed on the mechanic's shirt. It was *Wilson*. "This is going to sound insane, Wilson, but I need to get off this ship. I'm not supposed to be here."

Wilson took off his hat and scratched his head. "Well, partner, I'm way ahead of you on that one."

The door to the engine room popped open. Wilson snapped his attention away from Martin and turned toward the door.

Two men in uniform and a third one in civilian clothes walked to where Martin and Wilson were standing.

Speaking to the other mechanics, the tall officer said, "At ease, gentlemen." To Martin, he said, "Who are you, and how in blazes did you get on board the Eldridge?"

Martin briefly studied the three men, two naval officers and an engineer or scientist. Directing his answer to all three but focusing on the only civilian in the mix, he said, "Project Rainbow had a few side effects. My being here is an accident."

The men exchanged nervous glances.

"He looks a lot like one of the FC's—Fire Controlman Devereaux," the other officer said.

"Permission to speak?" the mechanic, Wilson, asked.

The tall officer gave a single nod. "Permission granted," he said.

"I noticed that, too. He looks like an older version of Devereaux."

"It would be better for everyone," Martin chimed in, "if you suspended the experiment and let me off the ship."

The officers stepped forward as if to apprehend Martin, but the civilian waved them off. "We're going to ask you again. Who are you, and how did you get on board?"

The scientist spoke with a slight German accent. Martin suspected he'd said too much already, opening himself up for all kinds of questions he probably shouldn't answer. He wasn't traveling the way he had before, something he needed to keep in mind. Now, more than ever, he had to consider that anything he said or did could alter the future in ways he couldn't understand. "The name is Martin Taylor, and I'm not entirely sure how I ended up here."

The scientist rubbed his chin. "Are you from another time and place? We will have a problem with zero reference points, won't we? You came to warn us."

Martin considered what he knew about the hideous results of the Philadelphia Experiment but remained undecided if trying to explain would help or make things worse. "Something like that," he said. "The whole thing was a big mistake."

The officers stepped forward and gripped Martin's biceps, forcing him toward the door. He suspected they would haul him to a detention area, where he would be locked away, trapped like an innocent prisoner as the ship went into hyperspace. "You don't want to do this," he said. "Things will go horribly wrong, both during and after the experiment."

"Wait," the scientist said. "I want to question the prisoner again."

The officers weren't liking it, but they paused anyway.

To Martin, the scientist said, "Okay, buster. Out with it. Tell me what you know. Is the experiment going to fail, or are you trying to sabotage it?"

Martin gathered his courage. "The magnetic field will cause the Eldridge to disappear for a few hours, but the nightmare begins when the ship comes back."

"Nightmare is a strong word. What exactly are we talking about here?"

Martin's stomach tightened. "The crewmen on board will come back disfigured, disoriented, even disembodied, tangled up with the fabric of the ship itself."

"My God. I suspected as much. Further testing is needed." He stared at Martin, pleading with his eyes. "Would you be willing to assist me with these tests?"

The tall officer tightened his grip on Martin's arm. "Doctor von Neumann, this is highly irregular. Everything is set and ready. The time for testing is over. We couldn't stop it now even if we wanted to."

"All right," Martin said, pausing as everyone turned in his direction. He had Doctor von Neumann convinced and had apparently instilled doubt in the lead officer. Martin was no scientist, but perhaps he could buy some time. "I'll help," he said. "Just tell me what to do."

Von Neumann turned toward the officers. "You are both familiar with my concerns. I have many times made them known to you. And now, the stranger confirms them. We can't go through with it. We are not ready."

The officer loosened his grip on Martin. "They intend to go through with this, Doctor von Neumann. At this point, nothing I say or do is going to change that."

"Please, Commander Ballinger. "I have feared this very thing," von Neumann said, "even dreamed of it. Please, Commander. We must stop the experiment, or we will suffer on our hands the blood of the inflicted crewmen."

"How," Commander Ballinger asked, speaking mostly to Martin, "could you possibly know this?"

"Because it happened," Martin said. "It's not exactly common knowledge in my time, but it's out there for anyone who takes the time to search for it."

Commander Ballinger brought his free hand to his forehead. "Well, that clears it up, doesn't it? It's already happened in *your* time." To von Neumann and the other officer, he said, "For crying out loud, gentlemen. The prisoner is insane. We can't stop the experiment, especially not on the word of some time-traveling crackpot."

"No!" von Neumann said. "Time travel *is* possible. My research, as well as that of my colleagues, has all but proven it. And due to the unconsidered element of time, the experiment will go horribly wrong."

The officers tightened their grip and urged Martin forward, forcing him to climb the stairs.

"I'm sorry," Commander Ballinger said. "It's too late to stop it now."

Martin's limited options danced before him, offering no more than increased desperation. There was no getting around it. He was hopelessly lost in a place he didn't belong. With the opening of another door, sunlight blazed into his eyes, and he was shoved onto the main deck of the ship, somewhere near the front of the vessel. No longer would he have to worry about what his presence onboard the Eldridge in 1943 might do. It was happening.

What started as a small vibration quickly escalated into violent shaking.

Von Neumann and the officers glanced at one another and checked their watches.

Sweat oozed from every pore in Martin's body. The experiment had started before its scheduled time.

The look on Commander Ballinger's face said it all. He and everyone else on board had been set up. Ballinger nodded toward the door they had exited through and urged everyone toward it.

Twisting around, Martin dragged the officers with him, but before they reached the door, a bolt of lightning streaked through the air and exploded onto the deck, engulfing the Eldridge in a violent storm, electricity snaking through the air like blue serpents squirming for survival.

Martin saw his chance. The ship's railing was only a few feet away. In 1943, two crew members had jumped overboard as the Eldridge had been drawn into the magnetic bubble. Martin sprinted toward the railing.

Someone screamed, "Stop!" and then fired two shots in rapid succession.

As if someone had slashed a knife across Martin's back, pain arced through him, robbing him of his senses.

CHAPTER TWENTY-FOUR

Montauk, New York
Friday, August 12, 1983, 9:00 p.m.

Martin floated through time, catching distant glimpses of the storm happening around the Eldridge. The disturbing thought that neither time nor place mattered here pounded in his temples. Had he been caught in a time paradox brought on by his multidimensional traveling?

Thoughts of his family blossomed in his mind. Susan, Luke, and Krystal were gathered together in a hospital waiting room. He wanted to go to them, but the image faded, only to be replaced by that of Doctor Stewart laboring away at the old warehouse, repairing the time machine. Stewart would succeed and use the machine again. Martin understood this on a deep level, though he could do nothing about it at the moment, and that image also faded.

Martin suspected he was now trapped in the time portal, unable to manipulate it as he had before, destined to float for an eternity in his self-made purgatory.

As if in answer to a prayer, a voice spoke from somewhere in the void. "Martin, pull yourself together!"

Martin recognized the voice and immediately regained his traveling abilities. He wasn't sure exactly where he had traveled to, only that it was where he needed to be. He managed a weak smile. "I'm failing, Grandpa. The more I try, the worse things get. I can't even save myself, much less my family."

"Has your family ever doubted you, Martin?"

"No. Like young children, their faith in me, as misplaced as it might be, is unshakable."

"Martin, your heavenly Father also believes in you. Is His faith misplaced?"

Martin cleared his throat. "I guess not. I mean, it can't be, can it?"

"No, Martin. God's faith cannot, by nature of His being, be misplaced. To even consider such a thing is sinful. Now straighten your ass up! Don't make me do it for you. My grace doesn't even come close to that of God's."

The storm surrounding the Eldridge again grabbed Martin's attention, but as he returned to the time tunnel, he continued to hear the voice of his grandfather.

"There are two kinds of people in the world, Martin. Those who go out and get things done and those who wait for someone else to do the job for them. You can't drift through life like a log floating on a river. You must have purpose. Some people would disagree with that, but they are the ones who fail. You're not like that. So, reach down inside of yourself, find your strength, and get it done. It's really that simple."

Grandpa Frank's voice faded, and the time portal also dissolved.

• • •

Martin immediately realized where he was. He had dived off the Eldridge and was still in the water, deep beneath the waves, his lungs screaming for air. He did as Grandpa Frank had commanded. He found his courage. Then he tugged and kicked his way through the water, grasping the very substance of its fabric as if it were more solid than liquid, and pulled himself to the surface.

Searching for answers as he dragged oxygen into his lungs, Martin glanced around. Darkness extended in all directions, an impenetrable inky blackness, the sum of his fears— darkness, claustrophobia, and an inability to right the situation. He knew he was in the water somewhere near the Eldridge, but he had no idea when. He searched his mind for answers. While he'd been in the time tunnel listening to his grandfather, a random thought had drifted through his mind—The date of February 23, 2014. For some reason, that date didn't seem to apply to his current location, but it had significance.

A surge of water covered Martin face, and he quickly turned, swimming in a different direction toward the sound of waves slapping the shoreline. When the rocks touched his stomach, he dragged himself upright and walked onto the beach, and then collapsed.

His rest was short-lived. The sound of someone calling for help echoed through the darkness.

Martin scrambled to his feet. "Where are you?"

"Over here." The man's voice was nearly swallowed by the waves. "I can't keep going. I'm exhausted."

Martin stumbled into the water. His adrenalin was pumping, but it wouldn't last, and soon, his own exhaustion would take over. "Keep talking if you can."

"I'll try. Please hurry!"

With a half-stumble, half-dive, Martin threw himself into the water and fought the strong current, swimming as hard as he could toward the voice.

"Help!"

Wheezing in raggedly, Martin pushed on, and with the third stroke, his hand struck something. He had found him.

The man panicked, thrashing like a dog trying to scramble up a slippery slope.

Martin had no experience to draw on. Doing the only thing he could think of, he worked his way behind the man, forced him into a headlock and then squeezed hard enough to get his attention, even in his current state. "Calm your ass down, mister! Drown *me*, and it's over! Understand?"

The man nodded.

Like a wrestler fighting for position, Martin worked the man onto his back. "Do you know how to float?"

"I can't."

"Yes, you can. Just relax, arch your back, slowly kick your feet. We're not far from the shore. Just keep floating on your back, and I'll guide you to safety, okay?"

The man shook like a nervous Chihuahua, but he was trying. "Okay. Like this?"

Martin kept one arm around the man's neck and used the other to swim. "You're doing great. Just relax and kick your feet. We're almost there."

Soon, the man relaxed. His breath slowed. "I think I can make it on my own now."

Martin paused and let go. "Just follow me, okay?"

"All right. How far?"

Martin swam but proceeded slowly, listening to make sure the man was following. "We're close. Another hundred feet or so, and we should be there."

And then, from somewhere behind him, Martin heard another voice calling out. "Is that you, Al? Where are you?"

"Here," the man Martin had rescued said. "I'm over here. Can you swim toward my voice?"

The other man's voice came back, but it was muffled, unintelligible.

"It's my friend, Duncan," the rescued man said. "I think I can make it now. Can you help Duncan?"

Martin had nothing left in his tank, but he could not let the man die. He dragged himself into the water and swam into the darkness, toward the man's voice.

Finding Duncan didn't take long. He must have heard Martin rescuing his friend and followed them toward shore. He was in better shape—not as panicked.

"Okay," he said. "Just lead the way. I can make it."

When Martin reached the shoreline, he walked onto the beach and collapsed.

Duncan wasn't far behind.

A short time later, the beam of a flashlight cut through the darkness. "Name's Duncan Cameron," the man wielding the flashlight said. He shone the light on his friend. "This is Al Bielek. Could you tell us where we are?"

Martin took a deep breath, wondering how he should respond to the question. He knew where they were, but Duncan's question had just confirmed that Duncan and Al did not. Then again, it was a little late to be worrying about altering the timeline. It would be best to let them find out on their own. "Since all three of us jumped from the deck of the Eldridge into the water," Martin said, "my guess is, we're still in the Philadelphia Naval Yard." He paused before adding. "Just before we jumped, someone called after me and then fired several rifle shots. The last shot struck me in the back. I felt it go in. But now I seem to be okay."

"Let me have a look," Duncan said. "I don't see anything. Strange things happen on the Eldridge, though. My guess is, you just thought a bullet hit you. Something's been puzzling me and Al, though. You look a lot like Devereaux. Are you related?"

Martin considered his answer, deciding to keep things as simple as possible. "The name is Martin Taylor, and I'm just as lost and confused as you. So, where do you think we are?"

Duncan shook his head. "I don't know, but I think we're about to find out. Someone's coming."

Silhouettes of people carrying flashlights emerged from the darkness, advancing menacingly closer, methodically walking along the shoreline.

Martin's pulse quickened as he realized the strangers wore military uniforms. He scrambled to his feet, taking a protective stance a few feet in front of Al and Duncan.

The soldiers talked among themselves as their flashlights explored the faces of Martin and his friends. One of them stepped forward. He was armed with a pistol strapped to his side, but he had yet to draw the weapon. A word or group of letters was stenciled across his light brown shirt that read, *DARPA*. "Who's in charge here?" the soldier asked.

Without giving it much thought, Martin said, "We were on board the U.S.S. Eldridge. The ship got into trouble, and we jumped overboard to save ourselves. We're not quite sure how we ended up here on this beach, but we mean no harm. We apologize if we've intruded upon private property."

The soldier turned away and talked into a radio, a large contraption that disturbed the silence with loud, intermittent bursts of static and muffled voices.

Moments later, he lowered the radio and spoke to Martin and his friends. "You'll have to come with us. You're not in trouble. We just need to take you inside, get you cleaned up, and then ask you a few questions. Come along peacefully; don't cause any trouble, and everything will be just fine."

The soldiers surrounded the trio and then marched them along the shoreline in a northerly direction. With the three of them being detained by DARPA agents, it seemed history was about to play out, albeit with a bit of a twist due to Martin's intrusion. A deep-rooted fear that he would forever be trapped in time grew inside of him as a concrete bunker embedded into the side of a large sand dune came into view.

Moments later, a loud buzzing filled the air, and the bunker door popped open.

"Step inside," the lead soldier said.

Martin glanced at Al and Duncan before complying with the guard's instruction. With two guards who carried M16 military rifles standing a couple feet behind them, they didn't have much choice in the matter.

Once inside, Martin gathered his wits and took in his surroundings.

Dim red lights set into the ceiling illuminated a hallway that wound its way into the compound's interior.

"What exactly are you planning to do with us?" Martin asked.

He received no answer, just a gentle nudging from a guard.

A strong sense of determination settled over Martin as he followed the procession deeper into the interior of the compound. He had to get back to his own time to find Susan and Luke. Time and place were the only obstacles. Then again, he *was* a time traveler.

Approximately ten minutes into the march, at yet another door, the guards stopped and talked into the static-laden radio. Seconds later, the metal barrier swung inward, exposing a room that served as a landing for an elevator.

The elevator doors swished open.

The lead soldier paused and then turned to face Martin and his fellow prisoners. "After you, gentlemen. And be quick about it!"

A mixture of anxiety and fear swirled in Martin's stomach and spread through him like a tidal wave. The mood of the soldier had turned serious. The admonition to move quickly only added to the tension.

"Where are you taking us?" Duncan asked.

The guard didn't answer. He simply loaded everyone onto the elevator and punched a button. When the doors closed, the elevator started with a jolt, dropping quickly, picking up speed as it descended.

Martin's instincts were to brace himself against the wall for stability, but with guards surrounding him, he could not. He was reminded of a carnival ride, which Susan had talked him into taking, that consisted of a large pole with passenger seats positioned around it. It, too, had dropped like a rock. Martin hated carnival rides.

When the elevator jolted to a stop, the doors hummed open. Through the opening, a palpable darkness tainted the atmosphere.

The guards ushered Martin, Al, and Duncan off the elevator and into an expanded hallway. Much like the elevator landing above, the area branched off into more tunnels.

A few of the guards broke off from the main detail and forced Al and Duncan down one of the tunnels.

"Where are the guards taking my friends?" Martin asked, though he knew the question would go unanswered. "What's up with all the silence and secrecy? It's not like we're criminals, you know."

A shove from behind caused Martin to stumble forward, a not-so-subtle nonverbal command for him to walk down the other tunnel, away from where Al and Duncan had been taken. About fifty feet later, in front of a dark-gray door set back about two feet into the concrete, the two guards escorting Martin stopped. One guard unlocked the door while the other one waited and then shoved Martin into the room, locking him inside.

Acting on instinct more than any real hope of success, Martin immediately tried to open the door.

Sealed tight, it wouldn't budge.

He turned toward the interior of the room, and with his back leaning against the door, he studied the area—ten by fifteen feet if he had to guess, sparsely furnished with a twin-sized bed in one corner and a small desk and chair in the other. Of course, there were no windows. But what would be the point of looking at dirt—or whatever was out there—beyond the thick walls of concrete?

Not knowing what else to do, Martin walked to the desk, pulled out the chair, and sat down. Made of heavy-gauge metal, the desk had only one long, shallow drawer. Inside, he found a pencil and a writing pad but nothing else. Without giving the action much thought, Martin retrieved the pad and pencil and jotted down, February 23, 2014, the date he had thought of while he was in the time tunnel. As a student in school, Martin had learned that the simple act of writing something down helped to secure it in his memory.

Just as Martin scribbled the date onto the pad, the desk and chair quivered. The vibration had been so slight that he wondered if he'd only imagined it.

Then it happened again.

Seconds later, an intercom system crackled to life, breaking the silence in the room. "Welcome to Camp Hero."

Martin's chest tightened. He struggled to breathe. It was the same unnerving salutation He'd heard during his first experience with the time tunnel. Martin now recognized the voice as that of Doctor von Neumann.

"In the closet near the bathroom facilities in your room, you will find a fresh change of clothing. Before putting them on, please refresh yourself with the shower facilities. The escorts who guided you to your quarters will return in thirty minutes, and then they will bring you to an area where we will meet and discuss matters"

Martin glanced down at his dirty clothes. Von Neumann and whoever else was behind their capture were moving ahead with whatever they had planned for Martin and his friends, and they were not wasting any time. But why had von Neumann's insistence upon showering and changing clothes sounded so urgent?

Martin immediately thought of his belongings, the small number of items he'd had on him when Doctor Stewart had shoved him into the time machine. Perhaps the guards were waiting outside the door, and while Martin was in the shower, they would come in and search his clothes. But that made little sense. They could have searched him when they first apprehended him. Upon considering that, Martin didn't think it would be a good idea for them to see his phone. That kind of technology hadn't existed in 1983.

He stood and reached into his front pants pocket, where he always kept the phone.

The phone wasn't there. Neither was anything else, not even any spare change.

Martin wondered if he could have lost the items during his swim to shore, but it didn't seem feasible that everything would have fallen out. And no one had searched him—not that he knew of—unless it had happened while aboard the Eldridge. That didn't seem right either. He had become aware of his location rather quickly. The most plausible explanation was that his personal items had not made the jump with him.

He shook it off and strolled into the bathroom, which was separated from the main room by a wall with an arched doorway. Taking a hot shower and putting on dry clothes would feel good. The tiny shower reminded him of the ones he'd seen aboard cruise ships. He twisted the knob and waited until the water became hot. After stripping down, he stepped into the steaming water.

A few minutes later, he turned off the water and reached for a towel. In the closet area, he found a jumpsuit hanging from a rack, and just below that, in a small cabinet, one pair of white socks and a pair of boxer shorts, also white.

Martin got dressed, a little surprised that everything fit. Then he went back to the desk and sat down. An unusual thought drifted through his mind. Luxuries like eating and sleeping became so routine that most people hardly noticed them. However, there was nothing like having that pattern suddenly disrupted to bring those comforts to the forefront. He had eaten and slept in various times and places, but how long had it been since he'd experienced any kind of routine in real time? Could time, as most people understood it, even exist for someone like him?

Again, he wondered if he had perished in the crash with Doctor Stewart. And what about Stewart? Had he survived, or had they both passed on to experience their own brand of hell—a string of never-ending time jumps that pitted them against each other in a game with no winners?

Another question came to mind. If Stewart was dead, did he realize it? And would a dead man continue to stalk the living souls of those whom he had perceived as a threat to his grand scheme of purifying the human race?

A loud knocking on the door shook Martin out of his reverie.

The door swung open, and two guards strode toward Martin.

Martin got to his feet, peacefully allowing them to escort him from the room. It would do no good to resist, and going along with them might be the best thing to do. He needed to get back to his own reality, and the time machine purportedly in use at Camp Hero could end up being the way to do that.

CHAPTER TWENTY-FIVE

In an underground facility at Camp Hero
Friday, August 12, 1983, 10:30 p.m.

Even with the lack of light in this part of the compound, an expansive area near the elevator, Martin recognized the man. It was Doctor von Neumann. He had aged considerably, but that was to be expected. Martin hadn't seen him in forty years.

Von Neumann studied Martin and the other captives, Al Bielek and Duncan Cameron. Then he signaled for the guards to stand at ease but remain close.

"I've waited a long time for this moment," von Neumann said. "And I've been expecting Mr. Bielek and Mr. Cameron. But you, Martin Taylor, are a different story."

Another tremor, like those Martin had felt in his room, shook the compound with enough force to gain everyone's attention.

"You don't belong here" von Neumann continued, "and you weren't supposed to be on board the Eldridge. You're a mystery, Martin. As a scientist, I am both intrigued and bothered by that. I need some answers. You owe me that much. If not for me, you probably wouldn't have made it off the Eldridge, and even if you had, the guards here would have already locked you away, if not something worse. So, where, exactly, do you belong?"

Martin struggled to rein in his jumbled thoughts. It wasn't like he hadn't expected the questions.

"Broken Arrow, Oklahoma," he said, "in the year 2020."

A smattering of laughter spread throughout the room. Even Al and Duncan joined in.

"Doctor von Neumann!"

The voice echoing throughout the expanse had come from one of the tunnels. The source, a man who towered over everyone in the room by at least six inches, now stood a few feet away from Martin and the others. Unlike the guards, his jumpsuit had the rank of Captain displayed on the collar.

"I'm surprised," the captain said with a bit of a sneer, "that you are so jovial, given the circumstances." The tremors are getting worse. What do you intend to do about it?"

Von Neumann dipped his head. "I'm working on it, Captain Conley, but thank you for reminding me that we don't have much time. I trust you will help me escort our guests to the lower level."

"Of course," the captain said, "but first, I need to have a little talk with your new friends."

"That would be highly inappropriate."

"Have you forgotten that it's my job to interrogate all prisoners?"

"At this point, they are guests, not prisoners, Captain."

"The captain rested his hand on the butt of a .45 holstered at his side. "I don't need your permission."

Even in the face of the subtle threat, von Neumann rolled his eyes. He had undoubtedly experienced trouble with Captain Conley before.

We've been over this, Captain. The only way to fix the conundrum we've caused is to send Bielek and Cameron back to 1943 to destroy the generators. Now, if you will kindly assist me in getting our guests to the lower level, we will get on with it."

Martin's knees grew weak. Von Neumann hadn't yet realized that he had sent Al and Duncan back to 1943 once before. They had succeeded in shutting down the generators and collapsing the original time tunnel, but the tunnel had reopened when Doctor Stewart sent Martin to 1943. Now, not only did von Neumann need to resend Bielek and Cameron to 1943, but he also had to send Martin back to the right time—the date given to him in the time tunnel, February 23, 2014.

Suddenly, Captain Conley unholstered the .45 and took a defensive posture. "I've got a better idea, von Neumann. I say we get rid of the prisoners right now."

Von Neumann rubbed his forehead. "Have you lost your ever-loving mind?" he asked, his voice rising in pitch.

"As soon as you send them back," Captain Conley said, "we're all goners. Isn't that right, doc, what you're not telling us?" He paused and waved the .45 around the room. "All of this...and all of us...will cease to exist. That's what people are saying. I like my life here. I have a lovely wife and two promising kids. You want to end all of that? Well, I'm not going for it."

Martin fought back a wave of nausea. Conley wasn't completely off his rocker with his twisted reasoning.

"The only way that could happen," von Neumann continued, "is if your entire existence directly resulted from this aberration, time rift, or whatever it is we have created here. That is so highly unlikely it's not even worth consideration."

Captain Conley shook his head. "I'm sorry, doc, but that's just not good enough." He swung the .45 around and aimed it directly at Martin. "If the prisoners are the problem, I say we eliminate them—take them out of the equation."

Thoughts of himself and the other two travelers dying here in the wrong time and place, along with the implications of what that might cause, exploded in Martin's mind. "That won't work," he said.

Everyone looked at Martin as if he weren't on their level and was, therefore, out of line.

"And why won't it?" Conley asked. "Get rid of you, and we get rid of the problem. It sounds logical to me."

Conley's wild-eyed stare with his finger poised on the trigger said it all. The man was ready to act.

"All right," Martin said, "but killing us won't solve the problem because we will still be here. Dead or alive, we will still present the same problem. We don't belong here; therefore, our being here is disrupting everything. The only solution is to send us back."

Conley relaxed his aim and lowered the weapon, but only slightly.

And then someone else spoke. "Don't listen to him, Captain. Like the others, he's feeding us a pack of lies."

It was the DARPA agent who had appeared to be in charge when Martin, along with Bielek and Cameron, were discovered and brought to the compound.

Martin saw his chance. With Captain Conley temporarily distracted, he could blindside the man. His plan made absolutely no sense. Conley outweighed him by fifty pounds, and he'd already shown he was in no mood for negotiations. If by some twist of fate, Martin knocked Conley from his feet or even caused him to lose his grip on the .45, then what? The other guards would quickly come to the captain's aide. Regardless, if the big man landed a punch with one of those massive hands, Martin would crumple like a broken mannequin. But none of that mattered. Through the years, he'd wasted enough time indulging in the luxury of contemplation. It was time to act.

Martin cleared his mind. Then, like a rookie defensive tackle going for the quarterback, he charged Captain Conley with everything he had.

And like some rookie tackle starting his first college game, Martin got lucky. No one stopped him because no one expected it, and with no hinderances, he smashed into the big man, dropping him on the spot. The .45 fell out of Conley's hand and clattered across the floor.

Unable to resist his gameday success, Martin indulged in a short but deliberate moment of celebration, glaring into the eyes of Conley as if he were a fallen quarterback; and the .45 a football rolling across the field.

Conley remained on the floor, dazed into submission, and no one, not even the other agents, moved. For what seemed a long, quiet moment, everyone just stood there staring, caught in a cloud of disbelief.

Still trying to grasp the situation himself, Martin left Conley on the floor, walked over, and scooped up the fallen weapon. Martin didn't run the fumble in for a touchdown, but he did what was needed in the present situation. He aimed the .45 at the crowd. "All right," he said, "von Neumann, Bielek, and Cameron, go to the elevator and stay there. Everyone else, keep your hands where I can see them and move to the east wall."

Martin's victory celebration didn't last long. As he held the .45, wondering what to do next, a chunk of concrete fell from the ceiling and crashed to the floor.

Another tremor was rumbling through the compound.

Martin stumbled toward the elevator, where von Neumann, Bielek, and Cameron had gathered.

The elevator doors opened. Von Neumann shoved Bielek and Cameron into the car and leaped inside, but he held the doors open, urging Martin forward with a jerk of his head. "Come on!" he yelled.

Martin ran for the elevator. He was only a few steps away when he decided to lunge the rest of the way, hoping to use his body as a wedge to force the doors to remain open until he could squeeze inside.

Halfway through the lunge, Captain Conley stepped in front of the elevator, blocking the entrance.

With momentum from the lunge, Martin slammed into Conley.

The big man was ready this time. He stood his ground, grinning as Martin banged into him.

Martin stumbled but quickly regained his footing.

Captain Conley's grin quickly faded. He had noticed something about Martin that seemed to frighten him.

It dawned on Martin what it was. He still had the .45 in his hand. Somehow, he'd hung onto it. He aimed above Conley's head and squeezed off two rounds.

The captain ducked and rolled.

Martin stumbled forward, but strong hands grasped the fabric of his jumpsuit and dragged him back.

Twisting around, Martin brought the barrel of the .45 crashing down onto Conley's face. Quickly, Martin tore free from the man's grip and jumped into the elevator.

With the doors closed, the elevator jolted downward. They were going to make it.

Martin gathered his scrambled thoughts. "Doctor von Neumann, you've probably already figured this out, but the déjà vu experienced by Captain

Conley and the others is not just feelings but real memories. All of this has happened before."

"He's right," Al Bielek said. "Duncan and I remember the events, too."

Von Neumann rubbed his forehead but said nothing.

"We have to do it again," Martin continued.

An unreadable expression crossed von Neumann's face. "For forty years, I have waited, knowing that Bielek and Cameron would wash ashore. What's puzzling me is why I had no memory of you also being on board the Eldridge, that is, until you showed up here at Camp Hero." Von Neumann paused. "I'm the so-called *brilliant* scientist. "So, Mr. Taylor, where did I go wrong?"

Al Bielek stepped forward, a look of urgency creasing his forehead. "When Duncan and I shut down the generators during the hyperlink, the time tunnel closed. It was as if none of this ever happened." Bielek hesitated. Then he put his arm around Martin. "We're again faced with reliving the nightmare because our new friend showed up in 1943, which ripped it open again."

Von Neumann nodded. "So, how do we fix it?"

Martin thought of the paper he'd written on while in his room. He pulled it from his pocket and handed it to von Neumann. "After you send Al and Duncan back to the Eldridge on August 12, 1943, you must then transport me to February 23, 2014."

Von Neumann studied the paper. "I thought you said you were from 2020."

The elevator jarred to a stop, and when the doors opened, Martin cautiously stepped off. It was too dark to see. "I don't have time to explain. Where are the lights?"

"A few feet to your left," von Neumann said."

Martin shuffled along the wall, and when he found the switches, he began flipping them.

Nothing happened.

"Conley," von Neumann said. "He's cut the power."

"If Captain Conley knows where we are, he'll come after us," Duncan said. "We need to go to another section and find a place to hide."

Martin put his hand on Duncan's shoulder. "We can't let our nerves get the best of us. We have to get to the time portal."

"The machinery won't work," von Neumann said. "Not without power."

Martin turned away and began walking into the darkness. He didn't know if he was going in the right direction, but he had to do something. No one else seemed willing to take the initiative. "What about a backup generator? There has to be one."

"Yes, but Conley is a smart man. He will have thought of that, as well."

Fighting to retain a semblance of composure, Martin spun around. "So, what are you going to do...give up?" He paused, listening to the sound of his voice reverberating throughout the darkness. He had let his frustration override his judgement. Like it or not, he'd been thrust into a role of leadership. Leadership depended on trust, and it was hard to trust an angry person.

"I'm sorry, Doctor von Neumann. I shouldn't have said that. I think we're all letting our nerves get the better of us. If we're going to pull this off, we need to work together."

Martin again began walking into the darkness. Finally, having lost hope that someone would volunteer the information, he asked, "Am I going in the right direction?"

"Sorry," von Neumann said. "Judging by your demeanor, I assumed you knew. Yes. We should be getting close."

Several minutes later, Martin slowed his steps. The smell of burned rubber and overheated copper filled the air. "Be careful where you walk," he said. "I believe we've found it."

Von Neumann shuffled ahead. After a few seconds, he said, "Just as I suspected. The entire floor has been shut down."

"Where's the backup?" Martin asked. "And what about a flashlight? There should be one around somewhere."

Von Neumann rifled through some drawers and then shone a beam of light toward a section of the room.

The equipment all looked pretty much the same to Martin, but he followed the beam, stopping near what he assumed was a generator. "Is this it?"

"It is," von Neumann said. "But surely you don't expect it to work?"

Martin thought of Doctor Lambert, one of the pastors at his church, whose favorite catchphrase was "Lower your expectations and raise your commitment."

A smile crossed Martin's lips as he found the generator's control switch, a large lever with red arrows showing the directions for both *on* and *off*. Without hesitation, he grasped the lever and shoved it forward.

For a moment, nothing happened. Then, as if it had been delayed by built-in safety measures, the generator vibrated and hummed, sending electrical current throughout the system, and the entire room came to life.

Martin strode across the room and rejoined the others. "Where's the portal?" he asked.

Von Neumann motioned with the flashlight, letting it shine on a part of the machinery resembling a small arched portico.

Al and Duncan glanced at one another and then scrambled into the time portal.

"It's too easy," von Neumann said. "Conley would never be so careless."

"Just do it!" Martin said. "Set the date and throw the switch!"

"It's a little more complicated than that."

Martin's patience evaporated. He grabbed von Neumann's shoulders. "Do whatever you have to do, but do it now before it's too late."

Von Neumann twisted free and sat in a swivel chair where he began maneuvering around a console, typing on various keyboards, glancing occasionally at the machinery. Electrical current arced and streaked inside the portal.

Moments later, Al Bielek and Duncan Cameron faded. Then they were gone. Von Neumann had done it.

Martin stared at the empty time machine for a moment, letting his thoughts catch up with what had just happened. Then he scrambled into the portal. "Do it now! Reset the date to 2014 and send me back!"

Von Neumann swiveled around and busied himself along the console.

A muffled thudding, like that of hoofbeats, sounded in the distance. Martin cocked his head as the pounding grew louder. His heart lurched when Captain Conley and several of his henchmen spilled out of the darkness.

The men swarmed into the area, encircling it, weapons drawn. "Well, what do we have here?" Conley asked, swaggering toward the console. "Looks like I was almost too late. I'm surprised at you, von Neumann. Of all people, I thought you would catch on and understand what's at stake here."

"Throw the switch!" Martin ordered, shouting above the noise in the room.

Von Neumann's hand streaked across the console.

But just as suddenly, Conley and the guards steadied their weapons and fired.

Von Neumann fell forward, his body slumping across the controls.

Fire belched from the men's weapons as bullets flew out the barrels and rocketed toward the time portal.

It shouldn't have been possible, but nothing surprised Martin anymore. Hoping to avoid being shot, he hurled himself onto the floor of the portal.

Some of the bullets whizzed safely past him, but then pain arced through him, and everything went black.

CHAPTER TWENTY-SIX

Near the old warehouse in Tulsa, Oklahoma
Sunday, February 23, 2014, 7:00 a.m.

Someone came out of the darkness and approached, his feet crunching against the ground.

Martin's best guess was that it was Captain Conley.

Soon, a shadowy figure appeared and stood motionless, staring down.

Martin rolled over to his knees and, after several failed attempts, got to his feet. His legs shook from weakness, and he feared he might go back down. "Where am I?"

The question surprised Martin. After all, he already knew the answer. He was still in the compound beneath Montauk, Island, though it was cold, much colder than before.

The shadowy figure hesitated. "You're an interesting person, Martin, one who never ceases to amaze me. Your determination is admirable, though I'm afraid it's all to no avail."

Martin recognized the voice, and as his surroundings came into focus, he realized he was not at Montauk Island. He glanced down at the gravel road and then scanned the area, seeing the old chain-link fence surrounding the warehouse. Von Neumann had successfully sent him to 2014.

Pain shot up Martin's left side. As he instinctively reached down and touched the tender area, his visual attention remained focused on the shadowy person standing near him. Soon, Doctor Stewart's face came into view.

Conley's bullet had done the damage to Martin's side, but Stewart intended to finish him off. He had Martin—dead center in his sights.

Martin gathered his strength and steadied himself, standing as straight as possible. Losing blood had weakened him. The only thread of determination he could wrestle from his mind was the knowledge of more being at stake here than his personal safety. He decided to buy some time, possibly diffuse the situation. "I wish I could drag up some anger, Jackson, but the truth is I'm kind of glad to see you."

Stewart grinned but steadied his aim, zeroing in on Martin's forehead. "Even if I did share your feelings, I couldn't let such trivial matters stand in the way of destiny."

It occurred to Martin that he could attempt a time jump and arrive an hour earlier, but he'd ended up at this time and place for a reason. Doctor Stewart had finished building the time machine, but he had yet to use it. Now was not the time for running, not the time for hiding. And like the football player tempted to rerun the previous play, only to reject the idea at the last minute, he knew taking Doctor Stewart by surprise would not work the way it had with Conley.

"What happens next?" Martin asked. "After you've played your version of Adolf Hitler, then what?"

Stewart shrugged. "Well, I hesitate to afford you such a lofty status, but for the most part, you are the only obstacle I've encountered. With you out of the way, the sky's the limit, as they say."

"Don't be so sure. The trouble with your narcissistic idealism, which thrives on extreme loyalism to a common goal, is that eventually someone will come along believing their loyalty to society is greater than yours, and suddenly the elite becomes the common threat; the hunter becomes the hunted."

Stewart shook his head. "I must say I expected more from you than such melodramatic rubbish. If it's any consolation, I wish there were another way. I really don't want to kill you. Nonetheless, it's time to get on with it. I've become a pretty good shot through the years. You'll probably never know what hit you."

Doctor Stewart's rambling did nothing to decrease his focus. In fact, his eyes grew more intense.

The moment slowed to a crawl as Martin hit the ground, rolled with it, and scrambled back up. When he found his footing, he ran, not toward Stewart, but away from him. When, he reached the fence, Martin climbed, feet and hands pumping and thrashing, until he reached the top. Then he straddled the fence, dropped to the other side, and ran for the warehouse.

A short distance ahead, barely visible in the dim light, several animal-shaped silhouettes bounded forward. Low, guttural growls emanated from the pack.

The dogs.

Beads of sweat slid down Martin's spine, but he continued to stride toward the warehouse.

A stack of debris caught his attention. He detoured toward the trash, scooped up a broken piece of wood, and flung it at the dogs.

One of them yelped while the others slowed, but the pack continued, steadily creeping closer.

Martin fumbled through the scrap and found something more substantial—a four-foot section of pipe. Grabbing it, Martin mimicked the pack's tactics and continued forward, quickly dissolving the distance between himself and the dogs. Then, like rival gangs showing respect before the fight, Martin and the dogs stood in silence.

Martin didn't wait around to see what would happen. He grasped the pipe like a baseball bat and swung for the lead dog.

The pipe connected solidly against the dog's ribcage, dropping the animal to the ground.

Martin didn't stop to admire his handiwork. He ran for the door to the warehouse. Then he broke the padlock with the pipe, kicked the door open, and stepped inside.

In the dim light filtering through the dirty windows, Martin caught sight of an interior wall, part of an office perhaps, with a ladder attached. He tossed the pipe toward the sound of the pursuing animals and bolted for the structure.

Sharp teeth sank into Martin's calf muscle. He cried out in pain but kept moving, launching himself toward the ladder. When his hand closed around a metal rung, he uttered a prayer and grabbed the next step.

Soon, the rungs disappeared and he found himself staring into darkness. He ran his hand across the top of the structure to make sure there was a solid surface. Then he rolled onto the area, wondering about the dogs as he dragged air into his lungs. Martin had heard of dogs climbing ladders; he'd even seen as much on television.

He cautiously rolled closer and peered over the edge.

A few dogs sniffed the ladder and the air around it while others plopped down for a rest on the concrete floor of the warehouse.

Martin rolled onto his back and stared at the ceiling, quite a distance away, much too far to lend any help in escaping. The dogs had him trapped.

After a short rest, Martin crawled around the area, investigating his current location. The interior structure appeared to be an office. The door, which had a crude window that appeared to be an afterthought, was made of wood and occupied an area along the front, about six feet from the ladder.

The other two side walls and the back wall had rectangular windows that looked to be about three feet long and five feet wide.

Martin crawled to the rear wall, peered over the edge, and studied the window. He was no acrobat, but he was pretty sure he could hold on to the edge of the roof, bash the window with his feet, and land inside the office. However, unless he could quickly block the window, the dogs would follow him inside, which would only make an already bad situation worse. And even if he did seal the window, he would still be trapped. It was highly unlikely there would be any type of phone service hooked up inside the office of an abandoned warehouse.

On a whim, he checked his pockets.

He still had no cell phone.

With no other options coming to mind, Martin rolled onto his back and scanned the upper area of the warehouse. About ten feet above him, a track ran north and south through the building. A large cable and hook attached to a pulley system completed the apparatus—a hoist designed to move heavy objects from one end of the building to the other.

Martin thought of jumping, grasping the hoist, and climbing onto the track. The problem was, the system ran about six feet to the east, and the cable hung at a slight angle approximately two feet to the south. His chances of successfully completing the maneuver were slim.

The sound of footsteps grabbed Martin's attention, and he quickly rolled over and scanned the area below.

Doctor Stewart had entered the warehouse and now ran toward the stairwell leading to the basement. Once there, he would fire up the time machine for its maiden voyage, and Martin would be caught up in a perpetual time loop.

Martin's heart drummed an erratic beat in his chest. He felt lightheaded...numb...as if his breath was carrying him away. The next thing he knew, he was soaring through the air, buoyed up by a slowly moving river of time, his legs spread apart like crooked scissor blades; his right arm outstretched, reaching for the hoist cable, straining for survival. He must have scrambled to his feet, run for the edge, and jumped, but he didn't recall having done so. An image of the dogs flashed in his mind, followed by a vision of himself hanging from the hook like a tasty piece of meat. What then? The canines wouldn't easily tire of their game and run off in search of a more enticing adventure.

Pain jolted through Martin's hand, arm, and shoulder as his palm slammed into the hoist. His fingers wrapped around the hook, but the sudden stoppage of his freefall overcame his strength, and he lost his grip. As soon as he let go, he plummeted toward the animals.

Grandpa Frank's words blossomed in his mind. *Find your confidence, Martin.*

Martin had a small bit of luck on his side. Grabbing the hook had slowed his fall. If he hit the ground in a loosened state and went into a roll, he had a good chance of coming out of it uninjured.

Then again, he would still have the dogs to contend with.

What happened next was a blur in his mind, but at some time later, Martin was on his feet, bolting toward the basement stairwell. He wasn't sure what had transpired with his facing of the dogs. He had heard of such things, like a lone scout caught behind enemy lines, defying the odds by fighting his way through a group of enemy soldiers to escape and live to tell the tale.

Martin reached the railing and bounded down the stairs, wondering about the dogs. What had he done? He uttered a prayer that he had only frightened the animals. Then he opened the basement door and peered inside.

Doctor Stewart stood over the operating console, his hands moving swiftly across the controls. Safely within Stewart's reach, a handgun lay on the console.

Quietly stepping into the room, Martin ducked behind some electrical coils near the door. He glanced around, hoping to find something that might be used as a weapon against Stewart.

An electrical hum filled the room. Stewart had started the time machine.

As if he had merely sensed an intruder's presence, Stewart grabbed the handgun and started toward Martin. "You're like a pesky mole tunneling through my yard, Martin. Every time I think I've gotten rid of you, somehow, you pop back up again. You might have hit a dead end this time, though."

Martin glanced around. Doctor Stewart must have heard the basement door opening. Sure enough, Martin had backed himself into a corner. There was only one way out, and Stewart was blocking the exit. While Stewart gloated, Martin trembled, his body shaking as if the temperature in the room had plummeted to below freezing. The superhuman strength that had come over him in dealing with the dogs was gone now, used up like an empty bottle of energy drink.

Stewart kept talking—something about joining him and how together they could do anything—but Martin wasn't really listening. Surely Stewart had to understand that, given the chance, Martin would do everything in his power to reverse the damage Stewart had done.

It was then that a small current of determination formed somewhere in Martin's psyche. He could not see Grandpa Frank or hear his words, but for the first time Martin knew, without a doubt, that Grandpa's genetic makeup coursed through his veins.

The moment Martin realized the truth, the trembling stopped. But he was still faced with the problem of being trapped and defenseless. He couldn't just walk out and reason with someone who'd already lost his mind. He couldn't put his arm around Stewart's shoulder and ask him to stop and talk about this. Stewart would kill him before he ever got that far. But none of that really mattered because something had to be done.

Martin edged closer to the south wall of the basement and slid toward the coils. The closer he got, the louder the humming became.

For a moment, he took a couple of deep breaths and gathered his courage. A gap of about three feet between the wall and the charged coils drew his attention. If he kept his back pressed tightly against the wall, he might be able to squeeze through unharmed by the strong current of electricity.

The problem was, if Martin made it through, Stewart would still be there, and there was no guarantee that emerging from a different location would catch him off guard. Even if the plan succeeded, the gaining of a few extra seconds might not be enough to give Martin the advantage. Sweat trickled down Martin's face as he stood there for what seemed a long time, thinking over what might or might not happen.

As he emerged from behind the coils, Martin paused, unnoticed for the moment, nearly immobilized by self-doubt. He had to get to the time machine, and he had to do it now. He might not get another chance, and it was too late to turn back.

Martin took another step, clinging to the wall as he edged closer. And then he was standing in the shadows. He steadied himself, balled his hands into fists, took one step followed by another, and slowly came up behind Stewart.

Before Martin could blink, he found himself staring into the expressionless face of Doctor Stewart, who brought the handgun up and pressed it against Martin's forehead.

Like a school kid getting ready to sneak out of class and being caught by the principal, Martin stalled for time.

"Hold on, Doctor Stewart. I've been thinking, you know, about what you said, you and I teaming up and working together."

Stewart raised one eyebrow and pressed the gun harder against Martin's head. "Oh, I see. Is that why you were sneaking up behind me? You should know by now you're no match for me, not even a threat, really. I should just shoot you down like the pesky nuisance you are. Come to think about it, it's the only way, isn't it? With your quirky and mysterious way of traveling, always showing up in the wrong place at the right time, I can't risk letting you go, much less trusting you as a partner."

The coldness of Stewart's eyes and the finality of his words stirred something inside Martin, and a blast of determination overrode his fear. He imagined grabbing the disturbed lunatic by the throat and shaking some sense into him but realized the futility of such an action. If he failed, which he most likely would, Stewart wouldn't hesitate to put a bullet in his head.

"There's something you should know," Martin said. "I've been working with someone, a man who calls himself John Rainbow."

Stewart frowned, feigning disinterest, but a look of concern floated through his eyes. "Like you, he's nothing more than an annoying gnat."

Martin scanned the area, making a mental note of the location of the time machine and the operating console. Some screwdrivers and other tools were scattered about. Stewart had obviously been making some adjustments.

"Don't be so sure," Martin said. "As you pointed out, I have a way of showing up in the wrong place at the right time. How do you think I've been able to do that?"

Stewart didn't answer, but his expression showed he was thinking over the concept, wondering if it held any validity. He pressed the 9mm against Martin's head. "You're lying, stalling for time. I've lost my patience with you and your games. And I'm not just thinking about getting rid of you. I mean to do it."

"Consider this," Martin said. "Mr. Rainbow has been tailing you for a long time, and now, with my help, a lot has been accomplished. When you fire up the time machine, something other than what you expect will happen."

Stewart thought for a moment and then stifled a laugh. "Nice try but a little too vague to take seriously. You have neither the knowledge nor the wherewithal to interfere with my traveling, much less the courage to pull off such a thing."

Martin had to concentrate and remember his mission. He had to get to the console and disable the machine. "All right, then. I'll be more specific. Punch the button on your magic carpet, and your atoms will be scattered all over the universe."

That got his attention.

Stewart stared at him. Then, for only a split second, he glanced at the time machine.

For hours, Martin had wondered how he might get to the machine and now, though completely unexpected, he had a chance.

Fear, not so much for himself but for what might happen if he failed to stop Stewart, fueled Martin's determination. He'd been in fights, mostly as a child, but he'd never gone up against someone who intended to kill him.

Years ago, Grandpa Frank, both during and after watching a boxing match on television, had pointed out what the winner was doing, and then he'd demonstrated the moves. At the time, Martin had not understood the relevance, but out of love and respect for his grandpa, he'd paid attention and sparred with his grandpa.

Even now, he recalled the basics, and he drew on that to prepare his next move. Pushed by a resolve so intense that he shut out all other thoughts, he stuck a stiff left jab into Stewart's face and followed it with a hard right hook to the ribcage.

To Martin's amazement, as reality once again set in, Stewart did not squeeze off a couple of rounds from the 9mm. He didn't even fight back.

He just stood there wavering, dazed for a moment. Then he grimaced and doubled over, dropping to one knee.

Martin stared at his opponent, not sure what to do next. Against the odds, he'd executed Grandpa Frank's moves well enough to disable the bigger man. The thought was quickly followed by another one. Stewart would not stay that way for much longer. He would recover and come after Martin with renewed vengeance. This realization, intensified by years of avoiding conflict, raced through Martin, threatening to derail him from what he had set out to do. He had to get to the time machine and disable it.

To gain a better position for the move, Martin stepped back and kicked the 9mm which Stewart still held. The gun flew from Stewart's hand and skidded across the basement floor, out of reach for the time being.

Martin spun around and sprinted toward the time machine's operating console. Licking his dry lips, he grabbed a screwdriver from the workbench he'd seen earlier. With the tool, he gouged and stabbed at anything within reach, bashing monitors and busting control knobs. Noticing an access panel, he tried removing it with the screwdriver, but the Phillips didn't fit. He needed a flathead.

A bead of sweat slid down his back as he glanced around to check on Stewart. Then he sucked in a breath.

Stewart was gone.

Martin quickly rummaged through the tools. When he found a flathead screwdriver, he scrambled back to the console and began removing the screws to the access panel. He'd gotten two out and had as many to go when a sobering thought crossed his mind.

Where was Doctor Stewart, and why wasn't he trying to stop him? A bit of logic dropped a load of realization on Martin, and he spun around, facing the time machine.

Stewart was stepping into the time portal, carrying an armload of papers. Once inside, he turned and simply stared at Martin.

No gunshots rang out, which probably meant the 9mm was still somewhere on the basement floor. If that was the case, Stewart had enough confidence that he was going to pull off making the time jump to have left the weapon behind.

Martin slammed his fist against the console before whirling back around. Just one lousy screw stood between him and the guts to the time machine. With trembling hands, he tried to thrust the tip of the screwdriver into the slot, but it slipped off. He was so shaky that he had to steady the tip with one hand and insert it. After loosening the screw, he tossed down the screwdriver and removed the access panel, flinging it aside.

Martin took in the exposed inner workings of the console in a single glance and tore into the circuit boards, busting them with the screwdriver while using his other hand to rip away the wires. The equipment seemed to be a mixture of both old and new technology, and it was then that the purpose of the papers Stewart carried became clear to Martin. Stewart had used his father's blueprints and plans to construct the machine, and he was taking them with him, not only to keep them out of Martin's hands but also to use in reconstruction, should that become necessary. An old-style calendar sitting atop the console caught Martin's attention and confirmed everything. The date showed February 2014. A red circle indicated the day as the twenty-third.

Martin grabbed a large wiring harness bound with zip ties and frantically yanked at it. The harness resisted, but when Martin leaned back and put his weight into it, one end snapped loose. Immediately, sparks jumped from the severed wires to the metal of the console.

He dropped the harness and strode toward the portal. running on an adrenaline-driven madness and hoping Stewart would not drag him into the glowing bubble, he reached into the portal and ripped a large portion of the papers from Stewart's grip.

Stewart glared at Martin. His mouth opened, as if to scream, but no sound came out.

Clutching the blueprints, Martin spun around and dashed to the console, where sparks were shooting out of the wiring harness like fireworks. In desperation, he shoved a couple pages into the path of the sparks. Soon, as he'd hoped, the papers blackened and smoked. Immediately, he leaned close and blew air across the smoldering material. As the papers burst into flames, he quickly fed the fire with more sheets.

The basement floor began to move.

Martin paused, wondering if he had imagined the sensation.

The ground shifted again, and the walls wavered like blankets blowing in the breeze.

It was happening, all right. Much like the other time fragments he had stumbled into where he didn't belong, the basement had become unstable.

Guided by a blend of instinct and intuition, Martin grabbed the handle of the portable tool bench, pushed it toward the time portal, and tipped the bench on its side. The tools clanked to the concrete and scattered across the floor. He then grasped the legs of the bench and, using all the strength he could muster, heaved it like a battering ram and plunged it into the wires connecting the portal to the console's controls.

The glowing bubble shrank, flickered, and then disappeared like a light bulb with a burned-out filament.

Doctor Stewart was no longer in the portal.

Martin stared at the empty time machine. Stewart could have completed a time jump, or he could be standing behind Martin, aiming the 9mm at his head. Despite the danger it might present, Martin hoped for the latter.

He dropped the tool bench, scrambled toward the exit. Then he flung the door open and stumbled into the stairwell.

The stairs pitched and rolled as if a powerful earthquake were rumbling through the building. Holding tightly to the railings, Martin took two steps at a time. When he reached the main floor, he ran toward the exit.

That strategy didn't last long. The moving floor took away his footing and dropped him to his knees, as if he were walking through a carnival funhouse gone horribly wrong.

Martin got to his feet, steadied himself, and then wobbled toward the exit.

Neither the dogs nor Doctor Stewart were anywhere in sight, but even if they had been, they would not have been Martin's only concern. The shaking of the building weakened the integrity of the ceiling, and chunks of it crumbled loose and crashed down like giant hailstones. The floor shook and turned to mush, grabbing at Martin's feet like thick mud. At a steadily increasing rate, gaping holes opened and swallowed the floor, the mush dripping into them like hot candle wax.

Not really wanting to but unable to help himself, Martin peered into one of the holes forming just inches from his position.

His stomach dropped as he stared into a never-ending darkness.

Steadying himself, he weaved his way around the holes and moved toward the exit. Pieces of the ceiling continued to rain down, and a large chunk struck his head. The impact blurred his vision, and a warm stream of blood ran down his face, but he kept going, driven only by the will to survive. At some point, with his exact position distorted by his fading consciousness, he smiled as cool air flowed across his face. He had made it out of the building.

Like a lost traveler unsure of where he was going, Martin trudged across what was left of the parking lot.

The terrain pitched, and the chain-link fence rose out of the ground, clinging to the fading time fragment like a stubborn old man who refused to leave his coastal home during a hurricane.

Martin Stumbled to the fence and smiled as he relaxed against the chain-link barrier surrounding the old industrial site. Guided by a higher force, his Father in Heaven, Martin had proved Tanner McIntosh's theory. He'd reached the point of origin and stopped Doctor Jackson Stewart from making the time jump that had reopened the rift.

Fire erupted and engulfed the industrial building. As the flames danced in the air, a black hole opened beneath Martin's feet, he fell, his stomach rising up in protest of the rapid descent.

Martin didn't see the building anymore or the parking lot or even the flames. He floated in darkness, a faint, familiar voice somewhere in the distance, calling his name.

CHAPTER TWENTY-SEVEN

In a room at St. John's Hospital, Tulsa, Oklahoma
Wednesday, May 06, 2020, 7:00 a.m.

When Martin opened his eyes, the first thing he saw was a blurry figure hovering over him. His heart lurched in his chest, his pulse quickening as he realized it was Susan, watching over him as one might do with a sick child.

A blank expression crossed her face, though it was accompanied by a nearly imperceptible flash of incredulity as she grasped the cross around her neck and blinked several times. "Martin?"

Martin immediately recognized his surroundings as a hospital room. He stretched his stiffened muscles. Then he reached up, though his arms were encumbered by wires and plastic tubes, and caressed Susan's cheek. He struggled for words, and when he spoke, his voice was hoarse and strained. "I love you," he said, "with all of my heart."

Susan's eyes moistened, but then her practical side took command. She turned away and raised her voice. "Get somebody in here!"

As if he had been standing just outside the door, a young man rushed into the room and dashed to the hospital bed, glancing at the computer monitors.

Susan stepped aside but remained close.

"Martin?" the man asked, looking at Martin. Seconds later, he added, "Do you know where you are?"

Martin suspected the young man was the nurse on duty. "In a hospital room," he said. "I was involved in a hit-and-run collision."

A disturbing realization washed over him. "What about Luke?"

Susan briefly removed her gaze from Martin and glanced across the room.

Martin turned and saw Luke get out of a chair and walk calmly to the bedside, a big smile on his face. "I prayed to God, and Mr. Rainbow came to our house. 'I bring him back,' he said. And he did."

Luke wasn't the only one who had stepped forward upon Susan's silent request. Martin's daughter, Krystal, was there, as well. She waited for Luke to finish before saying, "Hello, Daddy. You gave us quite a scare." She paused, choking back a sob. "I don't know how long it's been since I've told you how much you mean to me, but I love you, Daddy."

"Love you, too," Martin said. He had a world of things to talk about with Krystal, and he was as surprised as anyone at what he blurted out. "Whatever happened with Senator Padgett?"

A curious look crossed Krystal's face, as if she had a glimmer of remembrance, but just as quickly as it had come, it was replaced by a blank stare. She shook her head. "I don't know anyone named Padgett...or any other senators, for that matter."

Martin paused. Was it possible that Krystal had a vague memory of their rather unique experience and the meeting with Senator Padgett? Luke seemed to have a slight grasp of it. "You know, the abortion legislation, Luke, and the TV commercials."

Krystal's eyes filled with moisture as she shook her head and glanced at her mother.

Susan leaned over and kissed Martin. "Luke wasn't harmed," she said. "It was almost as if he hadn't been in the accident, except we know he was. Most of the impact must have been absorbed by your side of the car. Luke keeps going on about someone he calls Mr. Rainbow. His doctor thinks it's probably a delusion brought on by the trauma of the accident."

Martin winked at Luke but said nothing.

By now, several other people had gathered around the bed, doctors and nurses, Martin assumed. A short lady with gray hair, who introduced herself as Doctor Jeanne Larue, seemed to be in charge. She kept asking Martin the same questions the nurse had posed earlier.

"Yes," Martin said, "I know where I am and who I am. Now, let's get back to the accident. What about the other car? What about Doctor Stewart?"

A tear rolled down Susan's face. "There was no other car, Martin. You hit a light pole while heading north on Lewis Avenue near 51st Street. You must have blacked out."

"Doctor Stewart drove the big black car away," Luke said. "I no go back."

"Luke's right. Stewart deliberately hit us head-on."

Susan shook her head. "There were no other cars, Martin. Several eyewitnesses saw you veer off the road and hit the pole. What were you doing in that area, anyway?"

"Taking Luke to his appointment. We were both upset about it being on his birthday."

"I no go back."

"Don't worry," Martin said. "We're never going back to that place."

"There was no appointment, Martin. You and Luke were supposed to be on your way to the pro shop at Broken Arrow Lanes to pick up a bowling ball, Luke's present. The holes were being drilled. Needless to say, you were a long way from the bowling alley."

Martin started to say something but thought better of it. The doctors and nurses had kept quiet during his and Susan's exchange, but he suspected they'd been paying close attention and taking notes. He decided to drop the subject for now. His destroying the time machine had apparently changed a few things. "So," he said, "when can I bust out of this place and go home?"

"That depends," the short-haired lady who had introduced herself as, Doctor Larue, said, "on how badly your delusions are affecting you."

"What delusions? I hit a light pole while taking a rather strange detour to the bowling alley."

The doctor's face remained expressionless. "I'm concerned about your confusion over this *Doctor Stewart*."

"I no go back," Luke said.

Martin shook his head. "The name must have been in my subconscious for some reason."

"The police did question a Jackson Stewart," Susan said, "one of the eyewitnesses, a psychologist's assistant who works for the only psychologist in that area. He was very cooperative, checking the books and phone logs for the whole week. He didn't find anything about an appointment with Luke."

Luke shook his head, a hopeless look crossing his face. "I no go back."

"No worries," Martin said. "We have more important things to attend to. Candy has a birthday coming up."

Martin waited for a rebuke or at least some head shaking to his letting the name of *Candy* slip out, but none came.

"Well then," Susan said, "you'd better hurry and get well. It's coming up next weekend I believe."

"Next weekend," Luke chimed in.

Martin glanced at Doctor Larue. "What do you say, doc? Will I be free by then?"

The doctor's face softened. "If you continue to stabilize, I don't see a problem with that."

CHAPTER TWENTY-EIGHT

Tanner McIntosh's place—Candy's birthday party
Broken Arrow, Oklahoma
Saturday, May 16, 2020, 6:00 p.m.

Martin and Tanner sat in the same chairs beside the barbecue area where they had discussed the concept of time travel twelve days ago. Susan was near the house, happily engaged in conversation with Jennifer Barnes. Farther down the hillside, Luke and Candy played on the merry-go-round while several of Candy's friends swung on the large swing set and others scrambled about the various equipment.

A smile crossed Tanner's lips as Candy's laughter carried up the hill. He reached into the ice chest and pulled out a soft drink.

Martin grabbed one, as well. Tanner had changed little. He'd removed the beer from the cooler out of respect for his guests. Everything else seemed back to normal—no automatic gate and only one old Harley Davidson, tucked deep into the garage to protect it from being disturbed by anyone.

"Thanks for hosting the party," Martin said. "Luke looks forward to it every year, talking about the event weeks before and days after."

Tanner nodded, but his mind seemed to be on something else. "We need to talk," he said, "and the only way to get it off my chest is just to come out with it. I keep having this dream that you were here earlier in the month, on Luke's birthday, to be exact. You and I had a heated conversation that ended with us taking a bike ride on two old Harleys chosen from my garage. I have only one bike, Martin. And as far as I know, you've never owned one."

As if his last statement had been a question, Tanner paused and waited for an answer.

"No," Martin said, "I haven't."

"What's worse," Tanner continued, "is where we went and what we did there."

Martin twirled the soda can with his hands for a moment. "We all have unusual dreams now and then. I wouldn't worry too much about it."

As he said the words, he realized they were patronizing and inadequate, and he wished he had just kept quiet.

"We went to Oaklawn Cemetery, Martin. And I was mad as hell at you for putting me through that, making me look at Candy's grave because I had to show it to you. It's burned into my mind, and I know just as sure as we're sitting here that it's more than a dream."

Martin searched his mind for answers. How was he to explain such a thing? But there was no getting around the fact that Tanner had been pulled into whatever had happened enough to have residual memories. Trying to ignore it or skirt the issue wouldn't satisfy his curiosity.

"You're right," Martin said. "Luke and I got caught up in some kind of time loop. I involved you as well. I'm sorry. I didn't know who else to turn to."

Tanner's expression grew intense, and his eyes narrowed to slits. He opened his mouth to say something but stopped short.

Martin turned to see Luke running up the hill toward them. "Hey, Mr. Tanner. You like hummingbirds?"

Tanner's face softened. "Yeah, I reckon I do. Did you see one? It's a bit early for them, but sometimes they do that."

"Little Pegasus," Luke said. "We go to Florida. A vacation for sandcastles." He held his arms out like a child indicating something large. "A sandcastle for Pegasus."

After that, Luke turned and ran back to the playground equipment.

Tanner glanced at Martin, a puzzled expression crossing his face.

Martin finished his cola and put the can in a nearby trash bag. He could have taken the conversation in another direction, but for reasons he didn't understand, he thought he owed Tanner an explanation. "Luke has always been fascinated with hummingbirds," he said. He realized he couldn't remember exactly when the incident had taken place. He figured his confusion was caused by all he'd been through, but still, it bothered him.

"A few months ago, Luke, Susan, and I were prowling around an antique store. Not Susan's favorite thing to do, but for Luke's and my sake, she would never admit that. I found Luke mesmerized by one of those old Mobil Oil signs, the kind with the red flying horse on it."

"Pegasus," Tanner said, his eyes looking off into space as if he was trying to piece the story together.

Martin nodded. "I asked him what he thought about the sign. He held his arms out as he did a few minutes ago and said, 'hummingbird.' I knew right then that I had to get it for him. It cost more than I could afford, but Susan went along with it, never saying a word about it."

"I've met a lot of people in my lifetime," Tanner said, "but none better than Susan. You're a lucky man."

"Yeah. You're right about that."

Luke and Candy were running around with their arms out, acting like airplanes. They ran up the hill, and as they circled Martin and Tanner, Luke said, "I no go back."

Candy paused briefly, said something similar, and then ran after Luke.

Martin nodded. Candy was a bit overweight but had a cheerful face that always made him smile. "Every year, we vacation in Florida," Martin said, "and we build sandcastles, except Luke quickly loses interest and chases after Susan, helping her look for shells along the beach. Luke's talking about sandcastles is just his way of thanking me."

"Thanking you for what?"

Martin and Tanner's conversation stopped abruptly as a man dressed in a fine suit, as if he should be attending a high-level corporate meeting instead of a birthday party, showed up. He even wore a hat—unusual these days.

Martin couldn't remember him walking over. It was almost as if he had just appeared. Then again, that was exactly what had happened. It was the way Mr. Rainbow operated. Martin smiled. "Hello, John. Good to see you again…I think. What brings you here?"

Tanner sprang from his chair. He reached into the cooler but then came back empty handed and dropped the lid down. "This guy a friend of yours, Martin?"

"Something like that," Martin said.

John Rainbow tipped his hat before turning to speak to Martin. "We have much to discuss. But I can see now is not a good time. I'll try to be brief. During the conversation we had when you were stuck somewhere between 2014 and the time tunnel, our connection began to break up but not before you gave me the name of Doctor Stewart, a traveler Andrew and I had been looking for. I looked him up and paid him a visit. It appears you accomplished the mission. For now, everything is back as it should be. Job well done."

"Thanks, but I'm not sure I like the *for now* part. It sounds open-ended."

"Very astute of you to pick up on that. You have a rare talent, Martin, perhaps even unique. Andrew is quite interested in you."

"If Andrew's interest leads to anything like what I've been through, no thanks. And who is Andrew?"

John Rainbow said nothing. He simply tipped his hat and walked away.

Tanner's eyes looked as wide as the headlight on his Harley. "What was that all about?"

"Everything is back the way it should be," Martin said. "Perhaps we should just leave it at that."

Tanner shook his head. "Not a chance, Martin. A man dressed like someone's fancy butler shows up, talking about you and time travel like it was as ordinary as a walk in the park, and you expect me to pop open a beer—if I had one—and just forget about it. And that thing about not going back, Candy keeps saying that, too. Chris and Jennifer just blow it off. Like I said, Candy tends to ramble. But there's more to it than that, isn't there? You and I taking that ride to the cemetery was real. Candy was gone, Martin. And you did something that brought her back. You're not going to walk out of here like nothing ever happened. I want an explanation. You owe me that much."

The children's frivolity as they played vied for Martin's attention. The peace he found in listening to their laughter was overpowered by a fear he wanted to resist but couldn't—a fear triggered by John Rainbow's comments concerning Stewart.

"It's a long and complicated story, my friend."

"The party is just getting started," Tanner said. "I reckon we have a few hours."

Martin thought back to his waking up at St. John's. Susan had pointed out that the police had questioned someone named *Jackson Stewart*, an eyewitness to the automobile accident that had landed Martin in the hospital. The Jackson Stewart who the police had questioned was not a psychologist, but he worked for one. His life had followed a pattern similar to Doctor Stewart's.

As a warm breeze blew up the hill and brushed across Martin's face, he returned his attention to the children and their playing. They were happy because they lived in the moment, not worrying about the past or the future.

"We have a lot to talk about," Martin said. He would check on Jackson Stewart now and then. Perhaps Tanner could help. He'd expressed an interest in covert operations. "I believe the time is right."

About the Author

Bob Avey is the author of the *Kenny Elliot* mystery series, which includes *Twisted Perception, Beneath a Buried House, Footprints of a Dancer,* and *Identity Theft.* Through his writing, he explores the intricacies and extremities of human nature.

Bob is a member of The Tulsa NightWriters, The Oklahoma Writers Federation, and Mystery Writers of America.

Note from the Author

Word-of-mouth is crucial for any author to succeed. If you enjoyed *Sandcastle for Pegasus*, please leave a review online—anywhere you are able. Even if it's just a sentence or two. It would make all the difference and would be very much appreciated.

Thanks!
Bob Avey

We hope you enjoyed reading this title from:

www.blackrosewriting.com

Subscribe to our mailing list – *The Rosevine* – and receive **FREE** books, daily
deals, and stay current with news about upcoming releases
and our hottest authors.
Scan the QR code below to sign up.

Already a subscriber? Please accept a sincere thank you for being a fan of
Black Rose Writing authors.

View other Black Rose Writing titles at
www.blackrosewriting.com/books and use promo code
PRINT to receive a **20% discount** when purchasing.

www.ingramcontent.com/pod-product-compliance
Lightning Source LLC
Chambersburg PA
CBHW010735100726
47899CB00009B/3067